MW00944974

HONOLULU
HOSTAGE

A Novella ▪ Kay Hadashi

Honolulu ▪ Los Angeles ▪ Seattle

The Island Breeze Series

..

Island Spirit
Honolulu Hostage
Maui Time
Big Island Business
Adrift
Molokai Madness
Ghost of a Chance

Honolulu Hostage.
Book Two of The Island Breeze Series.
Kay Hadashi. Copyright 2014. © All Rights Reserved.
Second Print Edition, January 2021.

ISBN-10: 1501079158
ISBN-13: 978-1501079153

Cover art by author.
Cover images from pixabay.com.
Book design by Kay Hadashi Novels.

www.kayhadashi.com

Prologue

In the dark of night, and with nothing but confusion in her mind, June was stuck outside her home. She went from door to another, window to window, trying to find a way in. The rain poured from the sky, streaming down from the roof unabated, drenching her. What had started as a steady wind was turning into a gale, stinging her flesh, whipping her hair, tearing the clothes from her body. Every time she checked another window, it was locked against her efforts to find respite from the tempest. In spite of her desperation, she saw people inside, her family and friends, laughing, eating, singing.

She banged her hands against the window glass, shouting at the top of her lungs. The wind and the storm were too much for those inside to hear her. She looked up the slope toward the mountains behind her home, squinting against the rain. The same lights were there as always, as every time she was caught out in a storm. Torches flickered and flashed in the hills descending toward her. Drums hammered in the dark, rhythms relentlessly pounding. June banged her hands on doors and windowpanes again, hoping someone would finally let her in. She couldn't suffer this storm alone.

The rain fell ever harder, the wind ripped at her efforts. The drummers and torch carriers got closer, undeterred in their march forward. As they passed by the house, June cowered, hiding her face. One marcher stayed behind, and with the same message as always. There was no hiding this time.

"Ko-chan, you are in a storm again," her grandmother would say in old-fashioned Japanese.

Crouched against the wall of the house, June looked over her shoulder. The old woman was right behind her, watching her struggle. Seeing her so many times that way, in the dark, floating, footless, June barely cared that she was long dead.

"Bah-chan, tell them to let me in."

"Find your own way in, child."

"The storm...they can't hear me."

"They can't hear you? Or they don't know you're out here?"

"Maybe I've made too much noise already. Maybe the storm is too much this time. Maybe they no longer care."

June huddled closer to the wall, trying to get out of the cold rain.

"Don't blame the storm. You can stay out of the rain. You just need to learn how."

"I'm cold, Bah-chan. I want out of the rain," June said, whimpering.

"Instead of banging your hands, try turning the doorknob."

June cowered again, wind-driven rain pelting her frail body.

"Get up and try," her grandmother demanded.

June crept up to the porch landing. A shiver was setting in, her clothes soaked, her body wet, hair matted to her face, her eyes stinging. She reached a shaking hand up to the doorknob, grabbed, and turned.

The door swung open, light flooding her eyes. It was warm and dry inside.

June looked back at her grandmother, unsure.

"Go in, little one."

June took a step in, with as many tears on her face as rainwater. Endless gratitude buoyed her heart. She turned back. "Bah-chan...anji-jijo, domo arigatoh gozai--"

Her grandmother was gone, once again with the marchers, drummers, torch carriers.

The dreadful, hollow feeling stirred June awake.

Chapter One

That evening was the end of the first month of June's parents living with her on Maui. In the past, Sunday evenings were reserved for solitude, reading smutty romance, and getting a massage. But those days were coming to an end.

Her schedule as West Maui Medical Center's only neurosurgeon was getting busier, and the quiet time alone was her last chance to relax before the week started. Now in the second trimester, the symptoms of pregnancy were plaguing her days. Morning sickness till noon, crabby in the afternoon, evening cravings, and a headache from lack of caffeine all day long. Then there was her mother ruling the roost at home and a twin sister that mircomanaged everything else from two thousand miles away.

She needed an escape. If she couldn't have the solitude and unwind with a romantic cowboy named Trey, she could at least steal away for an hour for a massage. June dialed one of her favorite numbers. After making the appointment, she called out to her parents.

"Going for a walk. I'll be back in an hour or so."

"Evening walk?" her mom asked. "We could come with you."

"That's okay. A little peace and quiet would be nice."

The screen door slammed shut behind her. June got across the highway down the slope from her house and wound through the resort to the spa. She was there just in time to make her appointment, what she hoped would become her weekly escape from her parents.

"How's life treating you?" Dalene asked, warming the massage oil with her hands. The resort had handed out new uniforms for spa employees since the week before, the colors reflecting blooming flowers of the islands.

June was on her belly, her baby bump suspended in the knockout of the massage table. It wasn't just a massage, but a therapy session. "My parents finally got here."

Dalene lowered the cotton sheet to June's waist, and June adjusted her head position. She started with June's shoulders, her tightest muscles each week.

"And how's that working out for you?"

June winced as the working hands found the usual knot in her neck and worked deep. "One big happy family."

"And your mom?" Dalene asked, working her way down June's spine. "Does she like living here?"

"She likes managing my life." June turned her head to the side, sighing. "Or as she puts it, she's volunteered to take care of the house until the baby comes. And eventually become the nanny."

"Good for you!"

"It does let up some time, not having to make meals or clean. And I have to admit, I'm getting a little tired of my own cooking."

"Maybe a new cookbook?" Dalene suggested.

"Or a date in a restaurant with a guy, but fat chance of that happening ever again."

"It sounds like you're getting a lot of good advice about the baby," Dalene said.

"Between her, my dad, my sister, nurses at work, and my OB, there's no shortage of people handing out a lot of advice. But I have a good idea of who's going to be primary diaper changer when that time comes."

Dalene chuckled while holding the sheet aloft for June to turn over onto her back. "Yes, I suppose kids move out of the house eventually, for one reason or another, and most often it's to get away from mom and dad."

"Sounds about right," June muttered, luxuriating in the knuckle-rub an ankle was getting just then. Sometimes it was the littlest things in life.

"I finally had to sell my house out from under my kids, just to get them to move out. So far, they haven't followed me here to Maui." Dalene started on the other foot. "I was finally able to sleep, once I had some peace and quiet. Or not worrying when they weren't home on time."

"Sleep? What's that?" June mumbled between moans.

"Baby keeping you awake?" Dalene asked.

"I'm either hungry or have indigestion. Most of the time, as soon as I doze off, stupid dreams start up."

"Simpler foods and less oil will help with the digestion. Eat tiny meals all day, basically snacking. And you can blame hormones for the wacky dreams. Those will go away in time."

"I hope so."

"How's the job? Getting more patients these days?"

"Picking up a bit, slowly but surely." The massage had started on a hand, a knuckle being crushed into the pad of June's thumb. This was when the most pain came, but also the most relaxation after. "By the way, I won't be here next Sunday. I have a conference to go to next weekend on Oahu."

"Giving a talk on something interesting?" Dalene asked.

"Giving a talk, but I doubt it'll be interesting. Just the same old thing I always blather on about, the approach to third ventricle brain surgery."

"Ha! Whatever that is!"

"The best thing is I get to stay in an air-conditioned bed and breakfast for the weekend, and alone. I never thought warm weather would get to me like this."

"It's the pregnancy," Dalene advised. "The heat gets to all women during their second trimester. Don't worry about it. Just a few more months anyway."

June smiled. "Yeah, almost halfway there."

Dalene finished and helped June sit up on the side of the massage table. "Do you know yet if it's a boy or girl?"

June stroked her hand over her tummy. "No, just letting it be a surprise. Old-fashioned that way, I suppose."

"That's nice. That's the way it should be."

As soon as June was home, she was in the shower washing away the smell of the massage oil. Once she was out, she slipped into a T-shirt and shorts and found her parents in the living room watching an old movie on the television. It was a scene from decades ago, her father perched in an easy chair, her mother seated on the couch working on a craft of some sort.

"How was the walk, Dear?"

"Great. Nice weather."

They each took a stab at trying to remember one of the actor's name. As soon as her mother started in one the next day's meal selections, and how much June needed to eat, the relaxing glow she'd brought home from the massage began to recede.

"I'm going to bed early," June said. "See you in the morning."

Chapter Two

A common sight on the island of Maui was to see couples walking hand in hand on a soft beach, the bright sun tanning their bodies, the tradewinds sweeping past. Many of them were vacationers from far away; others were local inhabitants of the tropical Hawaiian island. Resort beaches with soft sand, swaying coconut palms, and gently breaking waves were the backdrops for romantic honeymoon moments late in the evening. In the early mornings, when beaches were mostly deserted, retirees and island residents would come out for spirited walks, quick jogs, or a few minutes paddling through waves before starting their days.

Almost as common were young local couples walking together, the woman obviously pregnant. In the early morning, some might have a blouse pulled snug over a baby bump, while others waddled along walkways past golf courses and resort cabanas. On this particular early morning, June walked alone. Her pretend husband was five thousand miles away, sham because they were married in a hastily-arranged wedding, which turned out to be officiated by an unlicensed chaplain. When he stayed in Washington DC to rule the White House and she moved to Maui to start a new life, the terms were set. Maybe they'd get married for real someday.

June wasn't holding her breath waiting for that to happen.

Only recently giving up her jogs, she wore only a black tank top, shorts, and rubber slippers. Arms, legs, and face deeply tanned, she tried walking as quickly as possible to get her exercise. Breaking into a sweat, she wiped it from her face with the back of her hand, knowing she had accomplished at least that much exercise.

"What's the use?" she griped as she slowed to a more leisurely pace. "My ankles are already watermelons."

She checked the time on her cell phone. There was just enough time to take one more lap to the far end of the resort beach and back again before getting ready for work. After turning around and making her way back, June was getting to the end of the long line of beach cabanas when she saw one of her surgical workmates coming out of the ocean, his surfboard under his arm.

"Hi Millertime. How are the waves?"

"Not bad today. Been out lately?"

"Had to give up surfing a few weeks ago. Surprisingly, OBs don't like pregnant ladies surfing."

He put the board in the back of his pickup. "Did you get the email about the new administrator coming on board?"

"Saw it. She has a bean counter background, which means she was hired to find ways of cutting costs and increasing revenue for the hospital. Hopefully she'll find ways of increasing my revenue in the process."

"Don't worry about it. You're doing as well as the rest of us."

"With my mom and dad staying with me now, I have two extra mouths to feed, and with the addition going onto the back of the house, there isn't much money left over in case…" She touched her tummy. "…there are complications."

"You'll be fine. You're healthy, you eat right, get exercise, and take your vitamins."

"I carry water in my ankles like a camel, sleep ten minutes a night, and can't keep food down. Since becoming pregnant, my life has become a festival of physical reactions. Maui really is paradise, unless you're pregnant and trying to sleep in an un-air-conditioned bedroom."

They sat on a bench nearby.

"Since you have that conference this weekend, you'll have an air-conditioned bed and breakfast to stay in," he told her. "But about the B and B. Maybe you should find a hotel room closer to the conference center instead?"

"Why?"

"First, there's the traffic in Honolulu."

"Taking a taxi everywhere that I can't walk. Plus, the B and B is just up the street from the medical center where they're holding the conference. Getting around won't be a problem."

"Kapalama Medical Center is in the Nu'uanu Valley, right?" he asked.

"Look, I doubt they'd hold a conference in a dangerous neighborhood. From what I've heard, there really aren't any dangerous neighborhoods in Honolulu."

"I've heard about the Nu'uanu Valley from someone at work. Seems it has a history." His expression turned serious. "Aren't you a little superstitious about ghosts and legends?"

"Maybe a little," June said. "I'm not a nut, though. Why?"

"The Nu'uanu Valley has several old cemeteries."

"I saw those on the map. I might go visit one or two if the weather is okay."

"Except there are some old Hawaiian legends about that valley."

June got a chill. "What legends?"

"First, that valley has been the site of several gruesome battles in the past. Then there's an ancient Hawaiian legend about the nightmarchers who inhabit the place. You should know by now the islands are full of legends and tales like that."

"I just know a few of the legends that go with Maui. What about the nightmarchers?"

"Just like all ghosts, they only come out at night and during certain phases of the moon. Pretty scary stuff to the Hawaiians."

"I won't have to worry about them, since I'll be at the conference during the day and back at the B and B in the evening. Just a short walk away."

"The Hawaiian Islands are not a good place to be superstitious," he told her.

"So I'm learning."

"They say nightmarchers are on this part of Maui," Millertime said.

June thought of the dreams she'd been having, and wondered if the books of Hawaiian legends she'd been reading had something to do with them. "I was reading about that a while back. They're supposed to be near here?"

He pointed toward the mountains opposite from the shore. "I was told they supposedly come down from there all the way to the beach." He gave her a dead serious look. "Your little house is right in the middle of their path."

June caught another shiver. "I didn't know."

"Anyway, back to daylight. Are you in the OR today?" he asked, going back to his truck.

"My first clinic appointment isn't until ten, so I might stay a few minutes and daydream about having a cowboy on a surfboard."

"Cowboy on what?" he asked.

"My latest Harlequin fantasy."

"I'm always available!" he said with a wave of his hand as he drove off.

She watched others surf long, rolling waves. The breaking waves were rather small that morning, the kind that she learned on a few months before. Just as she was graduating to larger sets, she became too pregnant to risk it. She liked being in the warm water, feeling the energy of the surf push her along, the slip off the board at the end of the ride, and the feel of sand on her feet. The sun would glint off the water late in the afternoon, her personal favorite time to be in the ocean. Her Asian skin had quickly tanned, her grown out pixie hairstyle now lightened by the sun. Even though her mainland-accented voice betrayed her, she was treated like a lifelong local resident by the people people she met. At forty years of age, there were too many risks involved with surfing for a first time mother-to-be. It didn't mean, however, she couldn't watch physically fit men plying waves.

In the bright sun of early morning, it was impossible to believe there were ghosts and spirits on these tropical isles. She couldn't set aside the eerie feeling she'd been left with after chatting with her favorite anesthesiologist at the hospital. It wasn't the best way of starting her day, before going to work as a neurosurgeon.

"The last thing I want to know is that there are ghosts in the neighborhood," she said taking a shortcut through the resort hotel property. She went past the same cabana she'd stayed in the year before, when she suffered a spider bite. There was the gift shop, and the main lobby, where she gave a wave to the same night shift receptionist as always.

Maybe it was the baby, or maybe it was the island ways catching up to her, but she felt new tenderness seeping into her soul. Maybe not gone, but the stern ways of dealing with people in Los Angeles were in retreat.

She followed the sunny path through the garden area at the front of the resort. Leafy green and purple ti plants and ferns decorated garden beds, palms shook in the growing breeze, and dramatic bougainvillea draped over rocky lava walls. Zigzagging through rental cars in the parking lot, she made her way to the road, her home across the highway from there.

"Probably why I got my house so cheap. Spirit zombies of West Maui, feasting on the flesh of marginally-employed pregnant neurosurgeons, walking alone in the early morning, her pheromonal sweat leaving an aromatic trail wherever she went, the dirty work of death being done by poisonous insects. And that's why I got the job of neurosurgeon here so easily. All the others were scared off." She chuckled. "Wimps."

***

"Hey, Dad. Is Mom up yet?" June asked when she went in the back door, stubbing her toe on a tool kit. "Do you need to leave all this stuff out?"

Most of her father's spare time and energy, and her money, were going into the new addition onto the back of the house. Since her parents had moved in, issues of privacy, boundaries, and routines were still being hammered out, as often as nails getting hammered into wood.

He moved his tool kit. "Just came in from watering the garden."

"Anything you can get done on the addition before I go to work? Maybe you and the tools could go find something to hit."

"Trying to get rid of me?" her father asked with a cheerful smile.

"Just want some girl talk with Mom, about the baby."

21

"I know that stuff too."

"Dad, you don't live here for free. Go hammer some nails in sticks of wood, okay?"

He smiled, putting his breakfast bowl in the sink. "You kids lived in my house for free when you were growing up."

"And we had chores to do every day. We even had chores at Granddad's house whenever we visited there."

"And look how strong it made you!"

"Dad…"

He wandered off, she heard muffled voices, and a moment later nails being hammered at the back of the house.

"Dear, how was your walk?" her mother asked when she got to the kitchen.

"Nice. Resort people apparently sleep late. Only the surfers were out."

"We can make that one of our regular routes, if you like. Dad said you wanted to talk to me about something?"

June verified with her mother what the obstetrician had said in her appointment the week before.

"Something about going to a young OB who's never been pregnant just seems off somehow," June said, wrapping up their conversation.

"But she said everything was okay?"

"She said I'm fine. I just haven't gained enough weight."

"I was a stick also, even your grandmother was skinny when she was pregnant. My father used to tease her about it." Her mother Mabel instantly stopped the conversation there, and June knew the reason why. Her grandmother had died while Mabel was still very young, and June never did get a good explanation about it. Right then, with ghosts and nightmarchers still fresh in her mind, she still didn't want to know. "What time will you be home from work?"

"Should be by six. Can you make something with garlic for dinner, please? I sense a craving coming on."

June passed through the Emergency Room, like always when she got to work, to see if they were busy. At the new West Maui Med, it was more of a 'Predicament Room' most days, a far cry from what she'd left behind in LA. It was the last day of work for that week, with a handful of clinic patients in the morning, and one surgery to do in the afternoon. Gone was her busy schedule before she moved to Maui, but having a quieter schedule right then while building up her new practice fit well with her pregnancy.

June centered her attention on her office computer, curiosity about Honolulu ghost stories getting the better of her. Scrolling through the internet, she found the site she wanted.

"Nightmarchers can be seen late at night marching down from the pali…that means cliff, right?…and into the Nu'uanu Valley where an ancient battle was fought. They can be identified by the torches they carry, but most often only those in their ohana can see them. Ohana means family, so that leaves me out. I'm not Hawaiian, and I'm pretty sure I'm the first of my Japanese ohana to live in the islands." She read about a battle that had been fought on Oahu many years before between two neighboring island armies, one of many battles. "If a person catches the gaze of a nightmarcher, they too are doomed to join them in their eternal march. The best way to avoid that is to lie on the ground and turn your face away, as if playing dead. Avoiding eye contact with a torch-carrying nightmarcher is most important."

Seeing several new Hawaiian words coming, she found an internet dictionary to help with the translations. "I should start learning Hawaiian." She continued reading down.

"On certain nights of the month, they return to battlefields or visit sacred sites. Marching just after sunset and just before sunrise, they often announce their arrival with chanting, a warning to others to run away until they've passed. Nightmarchers can also come during the daytime, to collect the spirit of a recently passed member of their chief's ohana. Since looking upon the nightmarchers is considered disrespectful and brings great trouble, showing respect to the marchers and their chief brings great reward."

She paused for a moment, looking at the artist renditions of the so-called nightmarchers, old Hawaiian warriors turned ghostly creatures.

"One common method of keeping a home safe from invasion by nightmarchers is to grow healthy, robust ti plants around the house and especially near the doors," she said, reading how to prevent Hawaiian ghosts from being disruptive. "I guess that's why the past residents planted all the ti plants around my house. They were as superstitious as me."

She read more about sacred plants and rites of the islands. Ti plants were always included.

"Hopefully the B and B will have them in the garden."

June noticed the time, and figured she still had time for one more internet article. She found a list of places that most commonly had histories with nightmarchers on Oahu, the island she would visit that weekend.

"All these Hawaiian names," she said to herself. "I have no idea where these places are. Kalihi Valley, Ku'aloa, Kapalama. Wait, the name of the hospital where the conference is located is Kapalama." She brought up a map of Honolulu on her phone and plugged in the name of Nu'uanu Valley. The Kapalama Medical Center was smack in the middle of it, and the bed and breakfast she'd stay at was nearby. "Great. I'm going to Grand Central Station for ancient Hawaiian spirits."

She read about a few other places on neighboring islands. The most common place on Maui was at the opposite end of where she lived, La Perouse Bay, a secluded rocky lava beach area she had visited once. Another place were the mountains slopes on West Maui, just like Millertime had said, exactly where she lived and worked. Next on the page was a link to 'ghosts of the Hawaiian Islands', which she ignored.

"Okay, time for work," she said, shutting down the computer.

***

"I hear you're going to Oahu this weekend for the neuroscience conference, June," Dr. Tran said. He was the anesthesiologist that was watching her patient in the operating room that afternoon. They worked together often, 'Transki' as he was called, an important part of the neurosurgery team that had been assembled for her. "Got a hot hunk of a lover going with you?"

"Ha! I wish! But are they still called hunks?"

"That's what the ladies call me."

June kept her attention focused on the ruptured spinal disc deep in the back of the patient in front of her. A long-time laborer, the man had not just one bad disc that needed to come out, but two. She held out her hand getting the proper instrument slapped into it by the scrub nurse. "Those guys on the covers of cowboy romances don't seem interested in me."

She wrestled with the disc for just a moment, but eased out a raggedy piece. Tiffany, the scrub nurse, wiped it away with a gauze sponge. June went back for more.

"How's the addition coming?" Transki asked.

"You mean the baby or the house?"

"Whichever is more important."

"This morning, I stubbed my toe on a tool box and nobody seemed to care, so apparently, the house takes precedence over the pregnant lady living in it. The new room is coming along, even if it is taking twice as long and costing twice as much as what I was promised. The baby is starting to kick, yet something else to keep me awake at night. I'm never quite sure if it's gas or the baby. My bladder is becoming a trampoline, and I've got enough water stored in my ankles for a trek across the Sahara. Otherwise, I'm discovering babies take twice as long and cost twice as much, just like home additions." She pulled out another small piece of disc, took up a syringe of fluid, and irrigated her small surgical worksite. She looked up and around at her workmates, rotated her head in a couple circles to stretch her neck. "Anybody here ever live on Oahu?"

"Not me," said Tiffany, another transplant from the mainland.

"I went to nursing school at the university there," Meredith said. A Maui native, she was the other nurse in the room, the circulating nurse as she was called. "Why? Need suggestions for cheap places to visit?"

"Actually, I'll probably spend most of my time either at the conference or at the B and B. Just curious about some of the history of the island."

"Like what?" Meredith asked. Her face had the appearance of so many races mixed together, something June had learned was called 'poi dog' in Hawaii. She had Asian eyes, dark Hawaiian skin, but was delicately-featured like Filipina women. Too much curly blond hair was mixed into her dark tresses, belying some European blood. "Lots of history there."

June got a stitch of suture in her hand and forceps to start closing the surgical wound. "Oh, well, the conference is at the new Kapalama Medical Center in some place called Nu'uanu Valley. I was reading about it a little, and saw something about nightmarchers."

"Yeah. Nightmarchers are really common on the islands. Mostly on Oahu and here on Maui. But I think people don't see them much anymore."

"That means some people have actually seen them?"

"Just the really spiritual Hawaiians. Some people are more receptive to that stuff than others. For everybody else, just something to talk story."

"I see," June said, cutting the stitch. She got a new one and started working closer to the surface. "It seems like there are a lot of ghost stories in Hawaii?"

"Too many," Meredith said. "Local people talk story about ghosts all the time. Each island has its own stories. So many battles in the past between the chiefs on each island, so much blood, so many people perished. Maybe those battles are long gone, but the stories aren't."

"People actually see things?" Tiffany asked.

"Orbs of light at ancient heiau, misty stuff in the woods, or they hear peculiar sounds in old houses. There's even some sort of night strangler at Schofield Barracks."

"A ghost strangler? Too weird!" Tiffany said.

"Wait," June said. "What sort of sounds?"

"I don't know. Creaky floorboards, the wind inside even when the doors and windows are closed. The usual, I guess."

"How do they get rid of them? I mean, is it possible to make sounds like that stop?" June asked.

"I think they just gotta live with it. That's why some people would rather live in a new condo than an old house. They don't want to deal with all the extra baggage that comes with the older places."

"They're all Hawaiian ghosts?" June asked.

"Oh, heck no," Meredith said, ready to apply the dressing. "Chinese, Japanese, Filipino, even Portuguese.

Maybe Japanese most of all on Oahu. Lots and lots of old Japanese cemeteries there, lost in the woods or simply forgotten. Developers there really have a hard time finding places to build on Oahu. Build on top of something sacred and watch out!"

"The descendants of earlier residents get mad?" June asked, watching as the dressing was applied.

"No. The ghosts of the past residents get mad, as in totally pissed off mad."

June sighed. "Swell."

"They were building Kapalama Medical Center when I moved here. I remember how there was all this anxiety in the news about the place, how no one researched the area before they started building, you know, a historian from the university."

"Too late now," June said.

After that patient, June's day was done, earlier than usual. She went back to her office, booted up the desktop computer, and plugged in a search term. Rather than satisfying her curiosity, listening to Meredith talk about island ghosts only piqued it. She read through several websites and university essays about ancient Hawaiian history, getting a primer on past kings and queens, and contemporary political movements toward native Hawaiian secession.

"This is way more complicated than what I thought," she muttered, turning off the computer. "More than just simple ghost stories."

Chapter Three

The next morning, June could smell her breakfast of burnt toast while she was still in the bedroom. She had eaten a large meal at dinner, having seconds for a change, and that morning was barely hungry for anything except coffee. That was something she'd have to sneak at some point when no one was watching.

"Is that toast mine?" she asked, seeing the black toast on a plate on the kitchen table. A glass of mango juice sat with it, which she felt to see if it had been chilled or freshly pressed.

"Is it dark enough?" her father asked.

"It's fine. The juice tastes good," she said, setting the glass down again.

"You want jam for the toast?"

"Do I ever?" she said, answering the same question he asked every morning. "Where's Mom?"

"Dressing. She already ate."

"Mom!" June called impatiently from the kitchen table. She pushed her second slice of toast away when her mother came through the kitchen door. "We need to go for our walk. I don't want to be late for my flight."

She knew her father would start frying an egg to eat as soon as they were out the door. It had become their routine, that he would cook while they were out on their walk, just so June wouldn't have to smell food cooking in butter. Not only was the aroma of burning food hard to take, but the scent of butter that it was cooked in turned her stomach. Now in her fourth month, she had expected the morning sickness to have eased, but not yet.

"Which way are we going today, Dear?" her mother asked.

"Across the highway and down through the resort. I like the beach down there, and there's always a bench available to park my expanding rear end."

"How are you feeling?" Mabel asked once they were safely across the two-lane highway.

"This morning? Like I hate life and everyone in it."

"The nausea will pass."

"I've been hearing that for weeks. Just like the caffeine withdrawal headaches were supposed to be gone by now, and I'm supposed to be sleeping better. Sometimes I think obstetricians get their training from racetrack handicappers. I should've bet on Lucky Eddie in the third race rather than get pregnant."

"Well, you'll get a change of scenery and an air-conditioned room for the next couple of days in Honolulu. You sure you don't want me to come along? I could drive you?"

"No. Not much for you to do there while I'm in the conference. I'm not getting a rental car just for a weekend. We don't know our way around there anyway. I'd rather take a taxi than get lost."

"I have blouses and skirts ironed and packed for you."

"If anything still fits."

"They were the loosest things I could find in your closet."

"Thanks. That boosts my spirits, that I finally have fat clothes to wear."

"You only show in your tummy…"

"And my hippopotamus ankles."

"Don't be like that, Dear," her mother said. "Pregnancy is something to be enjoyed."

"Maybe in the last forty years your memories of being pregnant with Amy and me have been idealized a bit, Mom."

They sat at June's usual bench overlooking the gentle waves washing ashore. It was where they often sat and talked, a family meeting place, or just a place to get some peace and let the breeze sweep her cares away. In the evenings there were sunsets to watch, the skies putting on shows.

"Too bad we can't go with you."

"Dad is already falling behind his work schedule on the addition. Having me out of the house for a while will give him plenty of time to get something done. Honestly, half the time I come home from work and it looks like nothing has been done that day. He's also spending my money faster than I can earn it. As it is, the five hundred bucks the conference is paying me to speak tomorrow is already spent."

"Your dad and I really do want to help."

"I know, and you're not going to. It's my house, my life, and it was my decision to move here. I'm forty years old, and I need to find my way through the world."

"Just like you always have. But you don't have to suffer."

"I'm not suffering, okay?" June tempered her voice. "Except for relentless morning sickness and a headache that started four months ago."

They watched as two early morning surfers took their boards to the water and paddled out.

"We'd like to help."

"You and Dad are helping out a lot. You're keeping the household together, and Dad's helping with the addition. I'm getting a lot of free labor, which in my book is even better than money. I have nothing to complain about."

"Except for morning sickness and a headache," her mother quipped.

June chuckled. "And swollen ankles."

After checking the time, they headed back home.

"How are the dreams? Still having them?" her mother asked.

"About Grandma? Pretty much every night."

"You really think it's her?"

"Same voice. Scolds me in her old Japanese inaka way like when Amy and I got too noisy when visiting them."

"But you don't see her?"

June knew it was her grandmother that visited her almost every night, deep in her dreams. She didn't have the heart to describe her as a ghost, choosing to keep the memory of her as a living person. June knew that if she were to begin thinking of her grandmother during rational daylight hours as a ghost, she'd lose sight of her as a real person so prominent in her life while growing up.

"I just know she's right around me, either giving me advice or scolding me. I don't know, but sometimes I wonder…"

"If she's upset you sold their house?"

They got across the highway after waiting for a gap in traffic.

"Yeah. Like maybe I disappointed them, that they feel disrespected that I let go of the Kato family home."

"I doubt that. If that were true, it would be your grandfather telling you about it. He and your father are just alike in that regard. If they think you've screwed up, they tell you." They trudged up the long gravel driveway that led to the house, a sweat breaking out on both of them. "Don't worry about your old house in LA. Anyway, you have a nice start on a garden in the back of yours, which your grandfather would appreciate."

***

Watching the local news on TV, June called for her mother.

"Mom! Got to go! Traffic is going to be a mess."

"What's wrong?" her father asked, coming into the living room wearing his tool belt, covered in sawdust.

"Accident on the highway going to town. Go hit a nail with your hammer, and not your thumbnail. Tired of hearing you swear."

"I'm getting better."

35

"You know you can't swear like that after the baby comes." She watched as he walked away, returning to his construction site at the back of the house. "I get the privilege of teaching the kid how to swear."

The accident scene on the highway to town was just getting cleared away when they got to it. Police were hurriedly waving cars through in both directions to get traffic moving again.

"You don't have to float O-Bon lanterns for your grandparents," her mother told June once they were on their way again.

"I know. But I'll miss the chance for lantern floating in Lahaina this weekend. I want to do it for them." June rolled her window up and turned on the pickup truck's pitiful air conditioning. "It's the least I can do."

"Stop feeling guilty. It was your house to do with what you wanted. If any of us really cared, we could've bought it from you. But a nice family lives there now. Time for you to move on."

"I want Grandma and Granddad to be with me, or at least memories of them. Anyway, how can I pass up the opportunity to go to O-Bon Matsuri at a place called Magic Island in the tropics?"

"Seems odd to have so many O-Bon Matsuri in one little place, and on so many different weekends in the summer. Our ancestors died only once," Mabel said as she drove in the practical way she always had, one of the things June appreciated about her. If only she'd press on the gas pedal a little harder. "Only need one lantern floating festival a year for them."

"The one on Magic Island is supposed to be the largest in the islands. But why the hospital decided to hold a conference on Memorial Day weekend, I'll never know."

"Good time for it. People have the time off to attend."

"Not hospital people, Mom. We're open for business 24/7."

Just as Mabel turned the car down the road to the airport, an airliner came in for a landing not far away.

"Don't worry about floating lanterns for your grandparents. They know you remember them," Mabel said. "Somehow, I think they've followed us here."

***

"Have a good trip," her mother said when she stopped at the departures curb at the airport. "Sure you don't want me to go with you? I could probably get a ticket for the same flight."

"I'm pregnant, not invalid. Why does everybody keep worrying about me?"

"You're forty, you're pregnant for the first time, you barely eat, you're stressed over the new house and money, and you barely sleep at night. Pretty good reason for us to worry about you."

"I get naps on my days off. And don't remind me I'm forty. I see the reminders in the mirror every time I look." She grabbed her overnight bag and took out her ticket. "I know my track record for taking care of myself hasn't always been so good, but I'm fine, really. My OB says things look good, just that I'm a little underweight. As soon as the morning sickness settles,

37

I'll be able to eat more. Believe me, I'm pretty sick of surviving on burnt toast, pretzels, and carrot sticks."

"You'll take it easy when you get there?"

"Taxis will whisk me everywhere. I'll give my talk, listen to a couple others, and hide in my room..." She smiled, and struck an advertising model's pose with an upturned palm. "...at Auntie Maile's Bed and Breakfast, enjoying the sensuous relaxation of the cool, lush Honolulu highlands, including a five-star breakfast and air conditioning."

Mabel laughed.

After a quick hug, June went off to check in, breezing through with only an overnight bag and her laptop in its carrying case. Once she was on the plane, she settled into the half-full flight and grabbed the magazine from the seat back pocket.

"What did she mean by 'followed us here'?" she asked, flipping through the glossy in-flight magazine. "They don't seriously think they're moving in with me, do they? It's busy enough having live parents in the house with me. Having a pair of ghosts in there might be too much."

Once she was at Oahu's airport, June reconsidered a rental car, but went to the taxi area at the airport, where she was lucky enough to get one right away.

"Auntie Maile's Bed and Breakfast on Mahalo Street in Nu'uanu," she told the driver once she was settled in the back seat.

He took off out of the airport and got onto the freeway headed toward town.

"Do we go anywhere near Magic Island?" June asked once they were on the highway.

"Back the other side," he said, jamming his thumb over his shoulder. He was an older Asian man dressed in an aloha shirt. "You want go Magic Island? Big mall near there."

"The bed and breakfast is fine."

June looked out at the scenery along the way, wondering if she had seen it before. She had done a couple of modeling jobs in Honolulu many years before, but never had seen much of the island.

"You just come from mainland?" the driver asked.

"Maui," she told him. From the back seat, she looked at the side of his face as he drove. He was a cheerful-looking man, she guessed Japanese descent, maybe about the same age as her father, only a tropical version rather than California-born.

"You look Japanese. What's your name?" he asked with the usual island accent.

"Kato."

He shook his head. "Don't know any Maui Katos. Know a Kato in Manoa Valley, up from university. That Kato?"

"No, I'm from Los Angeles originally."

"Here to see relatives?" he asked. "Show'em baby bump?"

"Medical conference at the new hospital. I give a talk tomorrow morning. But I want to go back to Magic Island tomorrow evening for the lantern floating ceremony. Do you know if that gets busy?"

He looked at her in the rear view mirror. "Oh yeah. Busy place all day tomorrow!" He handed her a business card. "Call me if you want a ride."

His card said *Ken Takahashi, Taxi and Delivery Service, throughout Oahu.*

Only a few minutes later, he slowly drove his taxi past the front entrance of the modern concrete and glass hospital where she would present her talk the next morning. Once the mini-tour was complete, he steered the van away and made a turn onto a residential street.

"This is Mahalo Street. Easy to get to the hospital from here, just few minutes walking. But careful walking after dark."

"Oh?"

"People say this neighborhood is haunted."

"Haunted?" June asked. It seemed to confirm what she'd read on the internet the day before, and what Meredith had said..

He lowered his voice as if telling a secret. "They built the new hospital on top of an old graveyard. They planned ahead and had the place blessed before they started building."

"They did that much, anyway," she said.

"Dummies got wrong kind of priest to do the blessing. These guys livin' around here know the results, and no so good sometimes."

He pulled the car to the curb, and June saw the sign out front for Auntie Maile's B and B. The website had made it sound bigger than what it looked. Instead of getting out, she waited a moment.

"And that was a problem?" she asked.

"Yeah. Got a Catholic priest. Then for good measure, they got an old Hawaiian kahuna."

"And it wasn't a Catholic or Hawaiian cemetery?"

"Buddhist. Just old Issei Japanese people in there that had the leprosy, long forgotten, but still..." He turned back to look at her when she paid for the ride. "They moved the gravestones to the Chinese cemetery up the road."

"And now..."

He nodded. "That's right. They think it was okay to just stick 'em in the back corner some place, like no one cares. But those headstones aren't the sacred things. It's the ground that's sacred."

"And now people think the neighborhood is haunted?" she asked.

"Maybe just around the hospital, where the cemetery was. But careful of O-Bake-san if you go out alone at night. These islands full of legends."

June thought of the vacation she had taken to another island a few years before, of some mysterious, and rather unexplainable, events with Japanese ghosts that took place then. "Thanks. I think I've heard a few of those old stories."

***

After being forced to drink a welcome glass of mango juice while she heard the house rules from the bed and breakfast proprietor, June was shown to an upstairs room. With the name of Auntie Maile for the bed and breakfast, she had been expecting Hawaiian ownership of the place, not a white couple from the Midwest.

41

"So, who's Auntie Maile?" June asked once she was in her room.

"The people in the neighborhood still call the place after the woman who used to live here many years ago. After her family moved out at the start of the war, a Filipino family lived here for a long time. When they moved out, a family from the mainland bought the place. But they didn't stay long after finishing a remodel. Then we turned it into a B and B. It's been very well-loved over the years."

"Sounds like it." June muscled out a smile at the woman, hoping it would be a signal that their little meeting was done.

"For breakfast we serve…"

"Yeah, something about that," June said to interrupt. She ran her hand over her bump in a circular motion to get the point across. "I still have a problem with morning sickness, which sometimes lasts all day. I'm not able to tolerate heavy breakfast foods, and I'm a strict vegetarian."

The woman looked at June and blinked.

"But I'm quite happy with burnt toast and juice."

"Burnt toast?"

"Burnt black, no butter. And any kind of juice is fine." June looked back at the woman staring at her, wondering if she had broken some sort of house rule already. "If that won't work, I can eat at the hospital cafeteria in the morning?"

"We have an excellent toaster, but I'm not sure it can actually burn something black. It's German made, so maybe it had burnt engineered out of it." The proprietor's face brightened. "And we have delicious Kona coffee!"

"As painful as it is, I'm trying to avoid feeding the baby caffeine. Is there a place nearby where I can get something for dinner? Something within walking distance?"

"How far is walking distance?"

"These days, a mile each way."

"Maybe a half mile or so down Liliha Street is a great bakery and restaurant. Grilled fish, beef stew, and the fluffiest pancakes in Honolulu. Open twenty-four hours."

On hearing about a beef stew, something stirred inside her belly, and June wasn't sure if it was hunger, indigestion, or another round of morning sickness kicking up. "Maybe something simpler than that."

"Just down at the end of this street is a corner grocery store. They might have something. And there's a little meditation center right across the street from it, if you're into that sort of thing. Some of our guests go down there for special sessions of something or other."

Once the woman abandoned June to the solitude of her small room, she got out her map and started searching. Sitting cross-legged on the bed, she found the neighborhood, and a small park nearby. Sure enough, a meditation center sat next to the park.

"Maybe they have a sitting this evening. Better than sitting around here anyway." She let out a gaping yawn while rubbing her swollen ankles. "Or just go to bed early."

The room was warm and stuffy. She had been expecting air conditioning, but as soon as she walked in the place, she knew it was too small of an operation to have central air. In the corner of her room was a small fan whirring, slowly moving back and forth. Taking off her blouse and khaki shorts she wore to travel in, she shook the wrinkles out of the shirt and draped it over the back of a chair to let the sweat dry. With the curtains drawn across the window and the light off, the dark room with the fan going, and dressed only in panties and a bra, she finally felt comfortable. Even the growing sensation of hunger couldn't keep her awake as she cuddled the pillow and drifted off to sleep.

Chapter Four

By the time June woke, the room had been cast into compete darkness. What had woken her was a grumbling stomach wanting something in it.

"I bet I've missed the sitting at the meditation center." Getting a bedside lamp on, she saw the clock. "I've been asleep for six hours? That's one heck of a nap."

She sat on the side of the bed, rubbed her face, and yawned. She checked her cell phone for messages and found a text from her father reminding her to eat something.

"Yes, eat." She tossed the phone aside.

Getting dressed and freshening up, she left her stuffy room behind. Downstairs in the living room of the bed and breakfast, she met the husband of the proprietor, along with the other couple that was staying there. They were looking in a picture scrapbook of some sort.

"I hear you only eat toast," the husband said with a cheerful smile.

June smelled something savory that had been cooked and eaten as dinner by the small inn owners. She smiled politely and looked at the four people looking back at her. Obviously, they had been gossiping about her. She needed to change the subject.

"What are you looking at?" she asked, looking at the open page of the scrapbook.

"Old photos of the house and neighborhood. Hasn't changed much," the woman said. The middle-aged woman looked June up and down a moment. "You might want to eat more than just toast, honey. That's not very good nutrition for a pregnant girl."

June stepped back, turning her eyes from the scrapbook to the woman. "Yes, well, I'm going out for a while. Maybe I'll find something more nutritious than toast."

She left as quickly as that. A few other people were out also, someone walking a fluffy white dog, a teenager skateboarding, and a jogger passed her, silent footsteps receding into the distance behind her. It was only a few minutes until she was at the corner grocery store.

June went up and down each aisle, wondering what, if anything, might stay down if she ate it. Evenings and late nights had produced the best results for her being able to eat, so she felt bold enough to get a tiny carton of ice cream, a vanilla almond flavor she'd never tried before. Along with that, she grabbed a bag of pretzels and a bottle of mango juice.

"Not much of a party for a Friday evening," the girl behind the counter said, taking June's money.

"Maybe next time I'll live it up with mint chip ice cream."

"Not like this place is Party Central."

"How's that?" June asked.

"Only stuff to do around here is go somewhere else."

June took her purchases, along with a small plastic spoon, and left the store. Uncapping the bottle of juice, she took a drink from it. Outside on the sidewalk, she looked across at the meditation center hidden by a large tree. A few women filed out, evidently the group that had met that evening for the meditation sitting. Once they had left in their cars, June walked across the street for the small park. There was only one bench, something that looked like it had been placed there by a family rather than a city park service. Scanning the area, nobody was around, so she sat.

The bench was cool to her bare legs. She stretched her legs out in front of her and draped one arm over the back of the bench. Almost immediately, a mosquito found her. She hated the idea, but she swatted it, and swept it from her arm.

"Sorry, but right now I need my blood more than you do."

By then, her cup of ice cream had softened. Tearing the bag of pretzel sticks open, she used them to scoop the ice cream out bit by bit. The salt of the pretzels was a tasty companion to the sweet vanilla and nutty almond flavors of the ice cream. A slight breeze settled over the area as she ate her simple meal.

She watched house lights come on one by one in the surrounding neighborhood. The street was quiet by then, the skateboarder done with his daredevil tricks, the little dog finished with its evening rounds of the neighborhood. The soupy ice cream was gone, and was sitting comfortably in her belly. June munched on a few more pretzel sticks, and washed each down with sips of juice. She set the pretzels and juice aside and stretched her arms over her head, twisting her back one way, then the other to loosen the kinks that had set in during her nap. It was the relaxation and solitude she'd been craving ever since her parents had arrived.

Folding her hands in her lap, she was ready to enjoy the evening, at least until she found two more mosquitoes on her arms. These she left to their simple meals.

"That's right, there's a creek around here somewhere," she muttered while rubbing her arms after the mosquitoes were gone.

From the corner of her eye, something startled her, movement as though someone was quietly approaching. All she wanted was to be left alone and enjoy the quiet evening. She snapped her head around to see who was coming. Once she saw there was little threat, she sighed and smiled.

"No reason to be afraid of me," the woman said to June. It was dark, and June couldn't see her face well. All she could tell from first glance was that she was middle-aged, maybe a little older than her, and some sort of dark-skinned Asian.

"Just startled I guess." June returned the woman's smile. She was wearing a dull brown yukata, a simple summertime style of kimono, just one thin layer to stay comfortable in warm weather. June's heart was warmed by the old-fashioned image of someone wearing a yukata after their evening bath, the way her grandmother had many years before. June pointed the lady to sit on the bench with her.

"Hapai, yeah?"

She was still surprised at the personal questions people asked, even hearing it from nurses at work a few times. She touched her bump and smiled. "Yeah. Almost halfway there."

"I no seen you here before," the woman said with a strong accent.

"I live on Maui with my parents."

"Come long way for see us," the woman said.

Seeing her face closer then, June could tell she was well into senior citizen years. "The taxi ride from the airport to here took longer than the flight."

"You're Japanese, yes?" the woman asked in old-fashioned *inaka* countryside Japanese, exactly the same as June's grandparent's accent.

"Yes, but third generation. I'm from California, actually. And you?" June asked back, continuing in Japanese.

"My parents brought us here when I was just a child. I've been here in this little neighborhood ever since, just down the street there. Can't imagine anyplace else."

"My name is Junko. Very nice to meet you," June said with a polite head nod.

"And are you?"

"Am I what?"

"Obedient, just like your name implies?" the stranger asked.

"Ha! Not always, I suppose." June picked up her bag of pretzels and juice to show the woman. "But I ate something this evening like I was told to."

"Not so much."

49

"More than some evenings. My stomach tumbles whenever I eat, at least things with any kind of flavor. So, mostly it's juice and bread."

A car drove past, June watching it recede around the bend in the road. Her companion gave it no consideration. Instead, the woman looked down at her hands in her lap. "I was never blessed with babies."

"Oh?"

"Not even married."

"I see." June looked away, suddenly self-conscious of her pregnancy. What she had been taking for granted would've been a privilege for the woman.

"Don't take pity on me for that. No one's fault, really. I just…I just never come out of the house much, not during the daytime."

"I'm glad you did tonight," June told her, hoping it sounded encouraging.

Her face brightened a moment. "Funny about friends, how they act when times are hard. Some stick with you, and others not so much."

"Relatives, too," June muttered. It was an odd turn in conversation, but she went with it. "Whether we want them there or not."

"You live with your parents on Maui?"

"They've recently moved in with me to help with the baby." June couldn't remember if she had mentioned she lived on Maui, but let it go. "Little house, and soon someone else will join the crowd. But we all get along."

They sat quietly for a few minutes. Just as June was wondering where the mosquitoes had gone off to, a falling star leapt across the sky.

"Pretty here," June mumbled, still looking up at the sky, watching and waiting for another miracle of a falling star.

"Should have seen it when we first came. The water in the streams was so clear, we played in it all day, looking for little fish. Used the water to wash our clothes, take bath, wash hair even. Always clean and cool." She let out what sounded like a forlorn sigh. "And then the disease came. Some died, others were just taken from their homes. We never saw them again. That's when my parents kept me at home, to keep me safe."

"That's sad, not to see your friends again."

The woman looked at June, with the fatigue of age in her eyes. "Yes, never again."

For the second time in their little conversation, the topic of friends came up. She too had abandoned her friends in a way only a few months before when she sold her house, quit her job, and moved away from them. She had stayed in touch with some friends, others not so much. She realized then that she had committed the same sin that had made the old woman so sad.

"I've heard this little neighborhood is haunted by ghosts, somewhere around here anyway. Do you know anything about that?" June asked after another pause.

"Old graveyard not too far." The woman waved her hand back in the direction of the hospital. "Seems like they're around, but benevolent. Nothing to be afraid of, but you won't meet many people out after dark. That's why I come out then, to be left alone."

"I see."

"You have a busy day tomorrow, Junko-san. You should get some rest."

"I suppose it's getting late."

They got up, and the woman went with June on a slow walk.

"You never told me your name?" June asked.

"Mari."

"Pretty name."

"Then later on, I got a new name. When the disease came here to plague the Japanese, the authorities took our people away, and left the others. They thought the Japanese brought the disease with us. But my parents gave me a Hawaiian name, just to protect me. Years later, once I was old, they just called me Auntie."

They walked slowly, June carrying the leftover trash from her simple meal. "Do you live near here?"

"Just up here, the green house. Big plumeria tree in the front."

"Just you, or is there someone else there with you?" June asked.

"People come and go."

It was getting tedious trying to wrestle clear answers from the woman, so June gave up on conversation and continued walking. "Thanks for talking with me. It was nice to hear about the history of the neighborhood. Maybe I'll see you again tomorrow evening?"

June turned to the woman walking with her, but she was no longer there. She stopped and turned around to look for her.

"Hello?"

She went back a few paces to where a tall hedge went from the sidewalk up to a house. Looking toward the front door, no light was on and no one was around. She looked around at the other houses nearby.

"None of these are green, and there aren't any plumeria trees." She shrugged her shoulders and went back to the inn. "Must've turned back."

She kept walking to the inn a few houses down.

"At least the Nu'uanu nightmarchers aren't out tonight."

At the inn, only the husband was still in the living room, waiting.

"Sorry I was out so long. It was such a nice evening."

The man locked the front door, and reminded June of the breakfast hours before going toward the back of the house. June still wasn't sleepy after her long afternoon nap, so she found a book to read in the little lending library in the living room. Unable to get interested in the story, she set it aside and looked at the scrapbook that had been left out.

She went back to the first page, and recognized a recent photograph of the inn, the husband and wife standing on the front porch smiling like proud new parents. A sign was in the yard, with Auntie Maile's Bed and Breakfast.

She flipped the page to find old photos of the house, both inside and out. It was obvious that at some point the house was added onto, that the original was tiny, not much more than a couple of rooms. As she turned pages, there was a succession of landscapes, a tree in the front yard growing up to be taller than the house. Then she turned one more page and the tree was gone, but the photo had become color. It was an older grainy image, and as she turned more pages, colors of the house changed with each new set of owners. There was one page of a white family, two parents and a boy, a bicycle leaning against a yellow hibiscus in full flower, a skateboard under his arm, a smile across his face. The next pages included pictures of a remodeling project, obviously taken by a modern camera. There were several loose photos of couples and individuals, some at the house, some taken elsewhere, all of them apparently guests at the inn. When she got to the last page, she quietly closed the book, turned off the last little lamp, and went upstairs.

June didn't care for reminiscing right then, especially over someone else's house and lives. There was something eerie about the place and she had a hard time keeping the old woman she'd just met out of her thoughts.

Chapter Five

June was downstairs early the next morning, as soon as she smelled coffee brewing. Even if she couldn't drink any, she allowed herself to enjoy the scent.

"Good morning," she said quietly to the woman getting breakfast foods ready. Nobody else was up yet.

"Help yourself to juice in the fridge. Sleep well?"

"Slept great. This neighborhood is quiet at night." June took a sip of commercially made mango juice, trying not to turn her nose up at it. She'd become spoiled by her father's freshly made fruit juice each morning at breakfast. "I was looking at that scrapbook last night for a few minutes. Nice that you keep alive the history of the house."

"Just a little hobby," the lady said, whipping eggs into a lather.

"How did you find all the pictures?"

"Oh, some were left behind. Others were given to us. A couple were from old newspaper articles."

"I see," June said. She leaned back against a counter to watch the woman prepare foods. Nothing cooking yet, so the aroma of oily food wasn't turning her stomach. "It's such a cute house. I wonder why the previous owners moved out so soon after remodeling it?"

The woman started grating cheese, probably for the egg omelets June suspected would be served at breakfast. "Oh. Them."

"Did something happen? Did they go bankrupt with the remodel? Not enough tenants?"

"You know that picture of them standing in front of the house?"

"The one with the boy, and his skateboard and bike?" June asked to verify. "That hibiscus certainly was preety."

"That boy died suddenly."

"Oh?"

What had started as idle conversation was quickly turning into gossip, but June had time, and since she wouldn't be eating much for breakfast, she may as well climb into the neighborhood grapevine.

The lady opened a small drawer in the corner of the kitchen and pulled out a stack of news clippings pinned together. June took them, glancing through quickly.

"Riding his skateboard late one evening, and he was hit by a speeding car. Not too far from here," the woman encapsulated.

June speed-read the article at the top. At the time of the boy's death, the new hospital was still under construction. Roadblocks were set up detouring drivers around the area. Police investigations determined the car in question never slowed driving through the quiet neighborhood. Too bad for the boy that perished, that he died almost instantly in the collision. The investigation wasn't even complete before the family put the house up for sale and moved away.

"That's very sad." June put the news clippings back in the drawer, suddenly disinterested in the history of the house. "I wonder…"

"Which upstairs room was his?"

June shrugged.

"We have no idea. One or the other. Both were completely empty when we moved in, both just painted white, no decorations, nothing. We never found any trace of a child that had lived in the house."

"And now he's dead."

"Funny thing, though," the lady said.

"What's that?"

"That hibiscus you mentioned is still there but hasn't had a single blossom since his death."

"That is odd," was all June could think to say."

"If you'd like to make your toast, help yourself," the woman said. "I'll start cooking soon, and you said smells bother you." She smiled at June. "I just can't bring myself to burn toast, even if someone asks for it."

"Sorry to be so fussy. It's just that…"

"That was me too. When I was pregnant, I lived on the food I craved and never ate anything else. Men just don't understand."

June dropped two slices of bread in the toaster and turned the setting up to the highest. "My problem is that I never have any cravings."

While she waited for her toast, she poured more juice, still thinking about the boy that had died, a recent resident of the house. Something about him and the image bothered her, she couldn't think of what. The toast popped up, a dark brown. She turned both slices around and shoved them down again for another round of burning.

"I think I mentioned I attend a conference at the hospital today. Just out of curiosity, how late can I stay out this evening before I get locked out? Sometimes people like to go out after conference meetings, do some networking, whatever."

"We generally have a curfew of around ten, maybe eleven if someone goes to a movie or show in town, and they let us know in advance. Just call if you'll be late and we'll figure something out. We worry a little if people are late coming back."

June took her toast and juice to the dining table. Settling in even before the table was set, she opened the newspaper and read while she ate. On the front page was an exposé article about the hospital where she would present that morning.

Local Hospital Rebuts Grave Claims

Lawyers for Kapalama Medical Center have once again countered a longstanding lawsuit brought against them with a suit of their own. Spokespersons for both Kapalama Medical Center and for the Foundation to Protect the Mizutani Cemetery indicated that settlement of the dispute is as far away as ever, and both lawsuits will proceed.

At the center of the dispute is the old Mizutani Japanese Cemetery, a one-acre site that held up to a hundred graves of long-passed leprosy victims. Five years ago, ground was broken to build the modern, state of the art Kapalama Medical Center, site of today's Interisland Neursoscience Medical Conference.

At the time, gravestones were moved to make room for construction of the building, a move that brought angst and clamor within the more established Japanese families of the island. Most concerning to the families was how the gravestones were handled, only that they were pulled free from the ground and carted away to another cemetery nearby. Only stacked in rows in a back corner of the old Chinese cemetery in Nu'uanu Valley, they have since gone disregarded.

Since that time, The Foundation to Protect the Mizutani Cemetery has brought one lawsuit after another against both the hospital and the general contractors responsible for its construction. No one can disagree it is too late to pull down the modern hospital building which serves a wide population within the community, but the Foundation's complaints also have merit. They wanted more respect shown for the graves, that they shouldn't have been regarded as ancient, since families of the victims are still within memory, and that nothing has been done to make final arrangements for the grave markers in their new location.

Both the hospital and the general contractor have made offers to arrange in "a respectable manner" the gravestones in their new location, and each time the offer has been rejected.

"Yeah, well, that's not going away any time soon," June mumbled under her breath. "Can't move an entire hospital, but did they really need to build it right on top of an old graveyard for lepers?"

"What's that?" someone said behind her. It was the husband of the couple that was staying in the other upstairs room.

"Hi," June said, looking up at him. "Just local politics that we can be glad we're not a part of."

He looked over her shoulder at the article.

"I saw something like that the other day. I guess it's this place right down the street from us. Imagine that, building a hospital right on top of an old cemetery. How's that for irony?"

June folded the newspaper closed and set it aside. "That's one word for it."

The wife of the couple showed up and sat. The table had been set while June read the paper.

"Are you here by yourself?" the wife asked. She glanced quickly at June's baby bump. "No husband to bring on vacation with you?"

June suspected the woman was shopping for more gossip. She wasn't going to share she had no husband. "I'm here for a medical conference at the hospital down the street."

"Oh, I see. You're a nurse here to listen to the doctors talk?"

One thing that always irritated June right from the very beginning of her medical training was when people saw her in hospital garb or a white lab coat, they would immediately assume she was a nurse or technician. Not that there was anything wrong with those occupations, but she had spent far too much time, money, and energy on her education and training to be confused with a different profession.

"No, I'm a doctor, here to give a talk for at the neuroscience conference."

"Yes, many women are getting into medicine these days," the husband said. "I suppose the next thing is that men will become nurses."

"What's your part in the conference?" the wife asked.

"I'm speaking on surgical approaches to the third ventricle with minimal loss of cerebrospinal fluid or surrounding tissue damage. It's a technique that I developed over ten years ago, something only a handful of surgeons in the world are willing to attempt. I'd like to see more surgeons here in the islands using it."

"Oh, that sounds so interesting! Hear that, Jeff? She's giving a talk."

"You're certainly welcome to come listen," June said. "I'm sure some men in nursing will be there to listen."

"Oh, I think we have something else better to do," the husband said with an insincere smile.

"I'm sure you do."

A platter of scrambled eggs was brought to the table, the scent of butter and eggs hitting June's nose and stomach hard. More plates of toast, a large bowl of runny oatmeal, chopped fried potatoes, and finally a plate of bacon arrived. Once June saw the oily bacon, her stomach turned too hard for her to remain comfortably with the others. Leaving one slice of her black toast and half her mango juice behind, she went upstairs as quickly as she could. Her stomach did somersaults the entire time.

She showered and dressed, and was ready to leave, even while the others were still at the breakfast table chatting. The morning sickness had mostly cleared while she showered, but once she was downstairs again, the heavy oily smell of cooked bacon lingered in the air.

"So, just down to the end of the street and over one block, and I'll be there, right?" she asked the owner of the inn. She had her grip firmly on the door handle, ready to go.

After getting a confirmation of the directions and a reminder to call if she was going to be out late, June left the inn behind.

She walked as quickly as she could, pretending it was real exercise, something that might push some of the retained fluid out of her ankles. As it was, she'd forgotten to put her feet up for a while before her shower. As the morning sickness subsided, hunger pangs took over, and she regretted not having the second slice of toast or more juice. But the quick walk in the warm morning sun felt good on her face, even if a sweat was building. In only a few minutes, she was in the welcoming air-conditioned atmosphere of the hospital.

Once there, she found the closest restroom to the conference rooms and freshened up. Back out again, she found the audio-visual tech that was responsible for managing visual slides that went with each presenter's talk.

"Hard to make a mistake with it," she told the techie young man. "There's only one file on my thumb drive, and it has my name on it. Just load it up and I can change the slides myself," she told him when she handed over her thumb drive.

"You should check in with Miss Chung so she knows you're here."

"And I can find her where?" June asked.

"Just listen for a loud voice out in the hall, then follow it. But she'll probably find you first." He was too busy organizing various thumb drives in a particular order to look up at her. "But you still have an hour or so before your talk. Just be back about fifteen minutes prior."

As soon as June was out in the main corridor through the non-clinical area of the medical center, she indeed heard a loud woman's voice echo down the hall, an Asian woman directing meeting participants into rooms.

"Must be Miss Chung," June mumbled, going in that direction. She could see the woman was demure in stature, nothing like the bold voice that almost bellowed throughout the commons area where she stood.

June stuck out her hand when she got to her. "Hi, I'm June Kato, one of your speakers this morning."

She barely got a slap of a handshake. "You were supposed to come by yesterday, just so I knew you were here," the woman said abruptly, without even so much as a smile or hello.

"Oh? I…"

The young woman rushed past June. "Come. Give your thumb drive to Paul so he can get it loaded up."

June tagged along behind Miss Chung. "I just saw him, and…"

"Then go to your meeting room and wait."

June watched as Miss Chung kept right on going to chase down other meeting attendees, looking at slips in their hands, pointing them off in different directions.

"Welcome to Kapalama Medical Center," June mumbled, going off to explore the hospital.

With time to spare, June found a vending machine that offered hot drinks. Getting tea, she poured half out and filled the cup with water. She looked through the glass window at a bag of pretzels, wondering if she should get some or wait. Preferring hunger over nausea, she forced herself away from the machine and back to her meeting room.

Once inside, she found one man already there, seated toward the front. He had his laptop on his lap, typing quickly. June landed in the first chair in the first row, trying to ignore what the man might've been doing on his computer.

"Are you here for the meeting?" he asked June without looking up.

"That's right."

"Still some time to go before anybody else shows up."

"Do you suppose there will be very many?" she asked, more curious about that than what she let on.

The room was smaller than what she had been expecting, more of a large classroom with rows and columns of individual chairs, rather than a horseshoe-shaped forum room she was more familiar with for conference talks.

"Not one of the hot topics. And first speakers of the day never attract many people."

"I see." She took a sip of her tepid tea, noticing her peach lipstick on the paper cup rim. "Maybe it'll just be you and me then."

"And the famous Doctor Junko Kato, neurosurgeon extraordinaire. Why they flew someone in from LA just for a little conference like this, I don't know." He continued to clatter away at his laptop keyboard.

"I think she lives and works on Maui these days. And I'm pretty sure her name is pronounced *Joon-koh*."

He looked up at her for the first time, and a grin crossed his face. "Don't tell me, you're Doctor Kato?"

"Brain surgeon extraordinaire. She got up and went over to him, shaking his hand. After he introduced himself as Doctor Barry White, newly released from his anesthesiology residency program in Honolulu, she sat a couple of chairs away, taking another sip of her tea. "Where are you working these days, Barry?"

He smiled at her. "Please, call me Doctor White."

"Okay." She took another sip.

"I have anesthesia privileges all over town and on two other islands, and do a lot of neuroanesthesia. I prefer private practice..." He was sure to put an emphasis on 'private practice'. "...hospitals downtown, right in the thick of it."

"I'm sorry, Doctor White, I'm not terribly familiar with downtown Honolulu. Is there a thick part as opposed to a thin part?"

"I meant figuratively."

"So did I." She reloaded right away. "You said you do neuroanesthesia. Have you done many third ventricle procedures, Doctor White?"

She knew he hadn't because there were still no surgeons in the Honolulu area doing those specialized procedures that might've taught him during his training. In fact, she knew every surgeon in the world that could do a third ventricle procedure competently, because she had trained them. But she also knew the reputations of many of the neuroanesthesiologists in Hawaii, from her medical journal reading and networking at large conferences elsewhere.

"Mostly, they're pointless. With so many cutting edge chemotherapeutic agents available, who needs surgeons? They should go into different specialties." He continued to tap away at his computer.

"Yes, maybe I should have. Why exactly are you here for this talk, Doctor White, if neurosurgery is so obsolete?"

"Licensure." He continued to type. "For continuing ed credits."

June got up and left him behind. She'd been around some pretty smug characters in her time, and LA medical centers had more than their fair share of them, but at least they had real-world experience to back up their attitudes. This kid had been out of training for barely ten minutes, and already he was passing judgment on other doctors' professional specialties.

"Are you Doctor Kato?" someone asked from behind her as soon as she sat elsewhere.

She turned around, unaware someone had come into the room.

"That's me." She stuck her hand out to shake his. "You are?"

"Doctor Andrew Lee, one of the neuro guys here at Kapalama Medical Center." He shook her hand vigorously, then opened his briefcase, taking out a paper office file. "I am so glad you're here this weekend. I have this patient in the ICU here…"

"I'm sorry, Doctor Lee, but I'm here to give a talk on third ventricle access techniques, not to do hallway consultations."

"Oh, but this is really interesting. It's a third vent procedure if there ever was one!"

He shoved a mini-X-ray in her hand while he gave a quick patient history. He took the X-ray back from her and held it up to the ceiling light. Dr. Lee was far too enthusiastic for nine in the morning on a weekend. Or too caffeinated.

He tapped his finger at a spot on the film. "Look here. The tumor is so large, it shows on simple skull films."

"That is impressive, but…"

She hadn't noticed before, but he had a full-sized X-ray jacket on the seat next to him, which he took to viewboxes mounted on the wall.

"Come look at these, Doctor Kato."

Begrudgingly, she went to the viewbox, her eyes quickly scanning the films, looking for the most important anatomical structures. She went from one film to the next, down the line of half a dozen, scanning and seeing with a trained eye, exactly as she had done a thousand times before.

"It's quite profound. What are her symptoms?"

As Dr. Lee went down a long list of signs and symptoms that June would expect in a patient with a tumor as large as in the X-rays, she noticed someone standing next to her. She looked to find Dr. White there, also looking.

"Doctor White, what do you think? Can chemo manage something that advanced, or should a surgeon resect first?"

"Depends on funding."

"Ah! Yes, somehow I thought it might. But if the patient has no insurance or funding?"

"Hospice care if her family is willing to pay. Otherwise, home care."

"And if she has full funding?"

"Resect to debulk, then aggressive chemo, followed by radiation."

She looked at the other doctor there at the viewbox with her. "Doctor Lee, does the patient have satisfactory insurance, enough to cover her care for something like this?"

"Just the state-mandated insurance plan."

"There you have it, Doctor White. You've doomed the poor woman to wait in line at the executioner's gallows. Maybe you'd like to go tell her the bad news?"

She turned and strode form the room, more because she needed the restroom than to bend the young doctor's ear any further.

Chapter Six

June nodded at the A-V tech to bring up the room lights and turned off the last of the slide show.

"So, are there any questions?"

She answered the usual questions, avoiding eye contact with both Dr. Lee and Dr. White. They both smacked of trouble, but for different reasons. Lee wanted her to work on a weekend off, and White had little interest in humanity. As soon as the two dozen meeting attendees filed out of the room, she turned around and heaved a sigh.

"Nice talk, Doctor," a woman behind her said.

"Pardon? Oh, thanks," she said back to Miss Chung. For once, the young woman's voice more closely matched her demure physical size. "Not as many people as I had been anticipating, though. How has the attendance been with the other meetings?"

"Good, actually. Each time we have a conference, attendance gets better. We're thinking of starting a monthly forum of sorts. Any chance you might be interested?"

"With a different neurosurgical topic each month? Maybe, but I have to come from Maui. That gets pretty expensive."

"We're also thinking of starting an online forum, a sign-up deal where surgeons from all over could participate."

"That's something I could do. I could use open clinic time."

"It wouldn't require much." Miss Chung held out an envelope to June. June knew it was the check in payment for her appearance, and tucked it away without looking. "Next time you come, I think we can find a colleague's home you could stay at."

"That would help with expenses."

Hungry and almost time for lunch, June went to the hospital cafeteria alone. Opting for something simple, she got the last bit of stiff oatmeal from the breakfast foods and a bottle of juice. Still too early for lunch patrons, she found a small booth in the back corner of the sunny atrium dining hall.

Between spoonfuls of oatmeal, she used a pen to jot a few notes on her napkin.

"Eighty dollars each way for the flights. Twenty bucks each way for a taxi to the airport. Twenty dollars for food. A hundred bucks a night for two nights at the B and B." She tallied the total. "Four hundred and twenty dollars to come here to earn five hundred. That leaves me an eighty-dollar profit. I need to manage these little junkets better if they're going to be worth the effort."

She sighed and dug into her cool oatmeal.

"Doctor Kato?" someone said.

She looked up to see a familiar face. The man was holding a tray of food with one hand, an X-ray jacket and briefcase in the other.

"Doctor Lee, have a seat."

While he sat, June grabbed her napkin with the expense tally and hid it away. The last thing she wanted was for others to know finances were a struggle right then. "Enjoyed your talk, Doctor," he told her.

"Please, just call me June. But I wonder what Doctor White thought?"

"He does seem more interested in the business end of health care," Lee said. He went about arranging his tray of food in a specific, almost neurotic, way.

"I don't have to work with him, anyway," June said, jabbing her spoon into the last of her hard oatmeal. She pushed away the bowl, bringing her juice closer.

"Given any thought to my patient, June?"

"Miss Tavares? The young woman with the tumor the size of a blimp? Really, I'm just here for the conference."

"Could you at least go see her in the ICU before you leave? I could have all the scans up for you to take a look, and you could do a quick chart review, jot a few notes?"

It was the oldest trick in the book, one June used occasionally, to coerce a doctor to go see a sick patient in the ICU. There was no better way of strumming the heartstrings than that.

"Andrew, I only have visiting privileges here at Kapalama. There really isn't much that can be done for the poor woman anyway. Surely the hospital won't allow surgery on her if she has almost no funding."

"I've already got the go-ahead from administration, that her surgical care would be written off as charity care, if I found a surgeon willing to do the complex case with me."

"And that means me, yes?" she asked. "Even if we planned something like this, it would take several hours, possibly up to twelve hours. With the extent of the tumor progression, I could only offer a twenty-five percent chance of survival. And that's ambitious."

He looked at her with large puppy dog eyes. "Are you going back to Maui today or tomorrow?"

"Tomorrow morning." She thought of the lantern floating ceremony as part of the O-Bon festival that she wanted to attend, and had heard about a large mall in town she wanted to visit, at least for window-shopping. She still had no maternity clothes, at least whatever eighty dollars could buy. "But I have things to do this afternoon, and they don't involve a long, complex surgery with a team I've never worked with before."

"You could bill as primary surgeon, and make it a teaching case for me and the others. Maybe if we work it right, we could do more of your third ventricle procedures here at Kapalama Medical, turn the place into a quality site for complex neurosurge procedures?"

That was exactly what she had done at Mercy Hospital in Los Angeles, help turn the facility from just an ordinary county hospital into a first rate neurosurgical center. It had taken several years of hard work, and she was able to pull from a base population of millions. The entire state of Hawaii had barely a fifth of the population of Los Angeles, a giant limiting factor.

"It would be nice to start something like that again. From what I've seen, Kapalama seems like a nice facility." She rested her hand on her baby bump, giving it a gentle stroke. "But I've got some other things on my mind these days, and I'm not sure about all the flying."

"You are pregnant, right?" he asked with a smile.

"Pretty obvious, I should think. I'm finding it limits my energy more than what I ever thought it would." She tapped her half-eaten bowl of hardened oatmeal. "Don't feel like eating much anymore, with all the morning sickness."

"No cravings?"

"It's the smells of things that put me off. The scent of cooking food…" June curled her nose into disgust.

"My wife had a hundred cravings, and they'd change weekly. When we married, she barely broke a hundred pounds dripping wet. I think she outweighed me by the time she delivered our first kid. Don't tell her I said that, though."

He got out his wallet and flashed a few pictures of his wife and kid.

"They look very sweet."

"Do you have other kids?"

"My first." She touched her tummy again and smiled. "This was a little unexpected."

"What does your husband do?" he asked.

That was a tough question, mainly because she wasn't married. The father was so prominent that his identity was being kept secret within the family. "He works back east in Washington DC."

"You want a boy or girl?" he asked seeming to process the information. June could only guess what he made of her answer.

"Personally, if I give birth to anything higher in the food chain than a lizard, I'll be happy."

It felt good to share a laugh with him right then, even if he was still a stranger to her.

His food was gone, and when June finished her juice, she glanced at her watch. She knew if she did a full consultation and workup of the young woman with the brain tumor, she wouldn't have time for shopping before the lantern lighting at Magic Island, the biggest activity left for her before going home again.

"I guess I could go see her," June said, giving in to some sense of moral duty. "But after, I'll need a ride somewhere, if you don't mind?"

"Didn't get a rental car?"

"Taxis everywhere. I'd be lost in five minutes time if I tried to drive in Honolulu." She smiled, wanting to offer an explanation for her ignorance. "I'm a child of the freeway. I figure if a freeway doesn't go to it, it isn't worth going to."

They left the table, tossed away their trash, and stowed their trays before going off to the elevators. "Where are you going later?" he asked, trying to juggle with briefcase and X-ray folders.

"Magic Island, wherever that is. There's a lantern lighting festival for O-Bon that I need to go to." June knew it sounded lame and selfish, that a festival to celebrate the memory of long-passed relatives should take precedence over doing surgery on a desperately ill young woman. "This is my first year here in Hawaii, and I feel pretty compelled to do something for my grandparents. I inherited their old home back in LA, something of the Kato family home, and recently sold it to move here. Doing that has made me feel like I've abandoned my grandparents."

"And you're now feeling a little guilty about it?" he asked, as they stepped into the elevator.

"Quite a bit, actually. And incredibly selfish. So, I'd like to do something that might make peace with them, if they're even paying attention anymore."

"I'm sure they are," Andrew said as the doors to the ICU opened. He led her off to one side, a sign hanging over a long hallway labeling the area as Surgical Intensive Care. "We have all surgical patients requiring intensive care in here, about half of our ICU services. Over on the other side are the Medical and Cardiac Units."

The department was larger than what she expected, and modern, with spacious glass cubicles arranged for each patient. Even at first glance, she could see a nurse at each bedside, not just sitting, but performing functions with the patients. She liked the place.

She read through the chart for the patient, Miss Tavares, and Andrew had given an accurate report of her. She went to the end of the chart, and sure enough, the woman had only minimal insurance. June also found a form, something called 'Suspension of Financial Obligation' from the hospital, the form indicating the

75

woman's services were being provided gratis. Snooping further, she found several social work notes for discharge planning, that the patient would go to a hospice center on Monday if surgery wasn't performed before then.

June performed a cursory neurological exam on the patient. She was unconscious and had the usual breathing tube in place, along with various intravenous lines and monitoring equipment. Because of the size of the tumor, her brain was slowly being crushed inside her skull, a condition that would soon lead to her death. Even her eyes bulged open a bit because of the displacement. Taking in all signs and symptoms of the woman's disease progression, June figured she wouldn't last more than another week or two at the hospice center.

She wrote a consultation note in the chart and slapped it closed. "Does she have family here?" June asked the nurse taking care of the patient.

"Her sister and brother-in-law are in the waiting room right now. One or the other of them is here around the clock."

She went back to where Andrew was waiting in a doctor's dictation room just behind the nurse's station. He had the most important X-rays up on a long viewbox, looking at them.

"How old are these scans?" she asked.

He tapped his finger on the date in the corner next to the patient's name. "Three days."

"I'd like to talk with the family, if you don't mind?"

He led her to the waiting room, where an exhausted-looking couple were seated.

"Are you Miss Tavares's family?"

The woman nodded, nudging the man with her awake.

June stuck out her hand. "My name is June Kato, another neurosurgeon. Doctor Lee has asked me to assist him in your sister's surgery. I have time today, if that's okay with you?"

Not only were they surprised, but Andrew Lee was also.

June sat with the couple while Andrew got the necessary consent forms together.

"She has almost no insurance, and we have little money to pay," the sister offered.

"That's not a problem. I think you already know the hospital has waived fees, and I can also, but you must realize…" This was always the hardest part of being a surgeon, when there was so little hope to offer. As a neurosurgeon, it was all too often that June had to break bad news to a family, that their loved one would be paralyzed and never walk again, or could very soon die from devastating brain trauma, in spite of her best efforts. All the technology in the world couldn't reverse much of what nature had already determined. "…there is only so much that can be done with the surgery. And even if everything goes perfectly, she might not survive the operation."

The young woman slumped where she sat, appearing even younger, even more unable to cope. "Doctor Lee said she might live only…" She used a tissue to blot her eyes. "…only another month."

"That would be optimistic."

"But Doctor Lee said there weren't very many doctors that could do my sister's surgery, and no one in Hawaii?" the young woman said. She looked very much like the patient, if she had been awake and healthy.

"It appears I'm the first in Hawaii. I've just recently moved here, Maui actually."

"You're so young. You know how?" the woman said in a deep accent.

June smiled, wanting to thank her for the compliment, but it wasn't the time or place. "I'm the one that devised the technique early in my career."

"Oh, you're the lady doctor from LA that everybody talks about?"

"I suppose so." June took a deep breath and slowly let it out. She wondered what had been said about her. As much as she enjoyed hearing meaningless gossip from nurses in the OR, she hated the idea that some of it might be about her. "I came to Honolulu this weekend for a conference, and that's when Doctor Lee approached me. I don't go home until tomorrow morning, so I have time."

There went window-shopping and lantern floating.

"And you can do surgery, I mean, like that?" the woman asked, glancing at June's belly.

"Not a problem at all. If there's any heavy lifting, Doctor Lee will do it."

The woman's eyes got big. "Heavy lifting?"

"Just a little joke we have in the operating room. Nothing in neurosurgery is very heavy, so…"

Andrew came back, rescuing June from further explanation. He had the woman, apparently the next of kin, sign papers.

After Andrew informed the nurse that surgery would take place that afternoon and to prepare the patient, June took him aside.

"This could be long. Maybe I should eat a little more and get some fresh air while you call the OR and make arrangements," she told him.

June went back to the cafeteria, hoping the aroma of lunch foods had settled. Taking a quick look at what was left, none of it would've sat well. Instead, she went to the snack shelves and grabbed a small packet of salty pretzels. At the checkout clerk, she handed over a couple of dollars.

"Nothing to drink with those?" the tiny Filipino lady asked.

"Maybe I should."

June went back to the drink station. Never being a fan of soft drinks, the juices also didn't beckon to her. All that was left was milk and coffee.

She grabbed a small cup and filled it with hot, black coffee.

"Sorry, Baby," she muttered as she walked out of the cafeteria. "This is the first day of your addiction to caffeine, and it has to be cafeteria coffee."

Chapter Seven

June took the front section of a leftover newspaper outside with her coffee. Finding a bench to sit on in the shade, she sipped her impulsive treat, the joy of caffeine almost instantly speeding through her body.

Deeper into the newspaper, she found another article about The Foundation to Protect the Mizutani Cemetery. This one wasn't much different than the article she'd read that morning over breakfast, giving the same background information. It went on to explain how the foundation had applied for a permit to hold the O-Bon Matsuri festival and lantern lighting on a place called Sand Island in Honolulu, but the permit had been denied by the city parks department.

"Lawyers for the Mizutani Foundation have already decried the decision to not allow the sacred ceremony to go forward, and hinted at the possibility of further lawsuits, this time against the city. The citizens action group that constitutes the foundation said they are considering holding the ceremony at Sand Island anyway. Now on the fifth anniversary of the desecration of the cemetery, the foundation is still as dedicated as ever in their pursuit of justice."

"I don't know if I'd call it sacred," June muttered, taking another sip of the coffee. "It's more like just something fun to do."

She finished the article, learning nothing new. She scanned a few ads for department stores in various malls in town, and looked over the local political topics in the editorials. The names and places might be different, but the same issues seemed to dog everybody. June refolded the newspaper and set it aside, taking another sip of the warm elixir called coffee.

Agreeing to assist with the surgery, her own plans for attending the festival on Magic Island that evening were now history. She suspected the surgery would take several hours, and wouldn't be out of the OR until late night, long after festivals were over. She thought about what the Mizutani Foundation complained about.

"Why can't they just go to Magic Island with everyone else?" she asked the gentle breeze that was kicking up. She slipped her phone out of her pocket and checked for messages. She tapped her finger on a number and waited. "Mom, I might take a later flight tomorrow. I'll let you know what time."

"Sure, Dear. Are you having a nice time? Seeing some sights?"

"Oh, yeah, seeing a few things."

"Get some rest before you go to O-Bon later, okay? And go to bed early tonight to get some sleep in the air conditioning."

"I will."

"Amy called, asking about you."

"Looking for anything in particular? Why didn't she just call me directly?" Her sister Amy was a bigger snoop than she was.

"Just checking on you."

"Just tell her there's nothing to worry about, which is true. Mostly." Normally her twin sister was also her best friend, but Amy had been micromanaging June's pregnancy which also meant she was taking privileges into managing the rest of her life. If Amy wasn't satisfied, she would drop in for a visit. The last thing June wanted was someone else coming. "Everything is fine."

June ended the call quickly. Looking at the time on her phone, she figured the patient should be in the OR by then, or at least close.

She hated to leave the breeze and sunshine behind right then, but she had a project to do. Going in a side door to the hospital, she followed the signs down linoleum corridors to the OR, her low-heeled pumps slapping on the hard floor. It was what she wore that morning to the conference, and with no other choice, would have to wear them for several hours of surgery instead of her comfy old sneakers.

Once she got to the OR, she saw the patient being taken in. June nosed around, but no one was at the front nurses' station of the OR, and she could hear activity in a couple of the other rooms there. For a weekend, it was a busy day in surgery.

She found the changing room, got some surgical scrub garments off a shelf and slipped into them. Stowing her clothes in an empty locker, she kept her phone and coin purse, before slamming the locker door closed. She looked down at the shoes on her feet.

"No, there's no way I can stand around in pumps for several hours." She tossed the shoes in the locker and put several layers of paper shoe covers on her feet instead of shoes. Standing, she tugged down the simple shirt to cover her tummy.

"I'll need a larger shirt pretty soon," she told herself when she looked in the mirror over the wash sinks. Loose at her shoulders, the thin shirt barely slid across her belly button.

The coffee was already kicking in by the time she was out of the locker room. She used a thin bouffant-style head cover, tucking in her hair all around. One last lock of honey-colored hair stuck out, which she swept under the covering.

June went to the room where her patient had been taken. Peering in through the window over the scrub sinks, she put on a surgical face mask and went in.

It was the same scene as always, nurses setting up equipment and instruments, the anesthesiologist managing medications and lines, and Dr. Lee putting up X-rays on the set of viewboxes. It could've been a scene in any OR in America.

"I see you found the locker room," said Dr. Lee when he saw her.

"Yep. But those shoes weren't going to work." She wiggled her toes inside the layers of paper covers.

June looked at the scans of the woman's brain, once again refreshing her memory of what needed to be done. She knew right off she'd have to make her standard surgical approach to get to the large tumor deep inside the woman's brain, an approach that was difficult to manage, even for her.

Another nurse came into the room to help the others. When June watched them for a moment, she got a shiver. Not from the cool room, but something else, she wasn't sure what. To distract herself, she refocused on Dr. Lee standing next to her. Even without shoes on her feet, she was noticeable taller than him.

"You want me to be primary?" she asked him. "I don't have my loupes or headlight."

"You can borrow a headlight. I'm not sure what we can do about loupes," the nurse said.

"I guess I could be primary surgeon," Andrew said hesitantly.

"Turning the flap isn't so hard, and the sulcus we need to tunnel past is easily identified with the approach I use."

"I like the see one, do one, teach one method of learning in the OR," Andrew said.

"Yes, well, we don't really have the luxury for that today. It might be a while before you get another one of these patients."

"True." His face burst with enthusiasm again. "Hey, let me introduce you to our crew today. Our scrub nurse is Gracie…" She waved and June could see the squinted eyes made by a smile over her mask. "…and our circulator is Sheryl."

"Hi. Nice to meet you guys. Were you on call today, and I made you come in?"

"Neuro call," Gracie said. "We only come in for neuro cases. But it's okay with me. I can always use the extra money."

June looked at Sheryl, who was busy positioning the patient's legs. "Personally, I had better things to do than this."

"And you've met Doctor White already," Andrew said, indicating the anesthesiologist. A technician was with him, and left the room with a tube of blood for a quick lab test.

"Oh, yes, Doctor White," June said flatly. It was the same guy that had insulted her specialty only that morning.

"Doctor Kato," he said. "Or should I say Joon-ko?"

"Doctor Kato will be fine."

"I guess I'll be able to see your fancy procedure up close and personal today. Even if I'm not getting paid for it."

"Consider it a part of your on-going continuing education, Doctor White." Talk of reimbursement in the OR was an unspoken taboo, and it always rubbed June the wrong way. Already irritated by the man from that morning's conversation, she decided to let it go. "And I'll be able to see your skills as a neuroanesthesiologist."

June went to the sterile table of surgical instruments, looking them over. She saw the basics of what she'd need. "Gracie, I'll use the medium-length blades on the retractor when we get to the brain, and mostly just a Number Four dissector, and then a skinny spatula and blunt hook from the microinstrument set. I'll resect the tumor with a small pituitary."

Gracie got those particular instruments out and held them up for June to see.

"Perfect! Otherwise, it's just the standard instruments on the scalp and skull."

It was coming time for June to get started with her own work. After checking the positioning that Sheryl had done, June went back to the X-rays one last time to double-check the name on them. Her last stop was at the patient to check her name band.

"How much of a bloodletting will this be?" Dr. White asked from right behind her while jotting vital signs on a sheet of paper.

June stepped away. "Bloodletting?"

"Will I need to transfuse?"

"Shouldn't be much. Mostly just from the scalp, as in any craniotomy. Why?"

"Just wondering how much blood I should have on hand," he told her, looking up at one of his monitors.

"It's standard operating procedure to have four units of red blood cells available for any craniotomy. We have that, yes, Doctor White?"

"Just wondering."

"Answer my question, Doctor. Do we have blood available for this patient?"

"Yes, everything is standard operating procedure, as you like to say, Doctor Kato."

"Thank you, Doctor White." It was a struggle, but she kept most of the snark out of her voice.

It was starting already, that deep feeling of regret for agreeing to do the case. The best thing to do was remain focused on the unusual needs of the patient. She turned around to find Dr. Lee looking at her. She gave him a tiny shrug and went back to the X-ray viewbox.

"I'm about ready to get started," Dr. White announced.

"Has a lumbar drain been placed yet?" June asked.

A lumbar drain is a tiny flexible tube inserted through the skin and placed next to the spinal cord to drain off fluid as needed during certain brain procedures. She got no reply, and figured it hadn't been since she heard a kit being opened and arranged.

"AS a qualified neuroanesthesiologist, you would've known to place a drain, especially after attending my talk this morning. You were listening, Doctor White?"

He didn't answer, focused on his kit of supplies. June watched for a few minutes as Dr. White tried to get the drain placed at just the right spot. The shaky movement of his hands made it obvious that he was struggling.

"Well, first of all, you started too high with your insertion point. You'll need to go one level higher on your next attempt," she said, watching from behind him. "They call it a lumbar drain for a reason."

He pushed his stool he was perched on away from the table and snapped off his gloves. "Maybe you can show us your technique?"

"If it'll move the case along."

June got a sterile pair of gloves from a cabinet, pulled them on, and sat on the same stool. Andrew was on the other side of the patient, holding her stationary on her side, with Andrew remaining behind June to watch.

"The biggest thing to remember is to get the right position." She had Andrew bend the patient's hips more, opening up the spaces between the individual vertebrae. "Find your landmark and make a tiny dent with a thumbnail. That's your insertion point."

She went on to explain the anatomical structures that he should feel for with his fingertips, and the angle of insertion of the large needle.

"As soon as you get a drop of fluid from the hub of the needle, feed the tubing through the needle up to the first large mark, and then carefully remove the needle and slide it off the catheter. Use two small silk stitches to hold it in place, along with some tape, hook it up to the collection set, and *Voila!,* we have a lumbar drain. Just be sure you keep it clamped shut until I tell you to open it. Draining off too much fluid too fast is a recipe for disaster."

She got it arranged on his side of the bed, helped Andrew and Sheryl position the patient again, and stepped back.

"Is there anything else?" Andrew asked. "I've read your journal articles about this a hundred times, but in the heat of the moment…"

"Everything just like for any other large tumor, but with the drain. We'll need to drain off some CSF when we get to that area of the brain, just to keep things fairly dry and workable. We just don't want to drain off too much or the third ventricle will collapse."

June went out to the hall to put on a loaner headlight and a pair of generic jewelry's loupes before starting the five-minute scrub of her hands at the sink. Looking through the small window, she considered the people in the room. There was Dr. Lee of Korean descent, the white Dr. White, the Filipina scrub nurse Gracie, and the very generic-looking Asian Sheryl. Without a last name for her, June couldn't begin to guess what races and heritages might be flowing in her blood. Stir in the Portuguese decent patient named Tavares, and Japanese American June, and it became a mini-UN summit meeting.

Between the enthusiastic Dr. Lee and Gracie, and the rather droll Sheryl and subtly hostile Dr. White, June suddenly felt stuck in the middle of something that she had no control over. What that might be, she wasn't sure. All she was sure about right then was the ominous feeling that it would be a long evening in the OR.

"Welcome to Kapalama Medical Center, June," she muttered dryly. "Thanks for helping out today."

She began scrubbing her hands and arms even more vigorously, almost angrily.

"I'm not going to let that jerk get under my skin. I'm not getting sucked into some stupid pissing match over the value of neurosurgery. I came here for a conference, and it's turned into doing a big case on the spur of the moment, and not even getting paid for it. If I'm working for free, I'm not taking lip off some clown ten minutes out of his training."

Andrew came out to join her at the scrub sink.

"Have you worked with this Barry character before?" she asked Andrew once he had a vigorous lather going on his arms.

"He's new to us. But he came with great references."

"Yes, well, sometimes a training center gives great references just to get rid of someone."

"I haven't heard any complaints," he said quietly.

"Personality clash, I guess," June said, tossing her scrub brush away, rinsing her hands and arms. With her hands up in front of her, water draining from her elbows, she went back into the room, pushing the double doors open with her butt.

Chapter Eight

They worked quickly and in unison at the beginning of the surgery, the time when there was the most blood loss. They had just got the round piece of bone cut and removed, and were looking to proceed with the more difficult part: working directly on the brain.

"As soon as we get the dura open, tissue will expand out the window we've made, Andrew. We need to work quickly to get our retractors in and tissue pushed aside. I've found I have very little tissue loss that way, if I go right through the sulcus, deflecting tissue apart rather than tunneling. But with the size of this woman's tumor, we'll need to reset the retractor a few times as we debulk our way deeper."

Andrew was working in the position of assistant surgeon. "I've read about how you use the Golden Ratio as a template for finding your starting point, and your slides this morning were great. I'm just so reluctant to find that specific point."

"I used to use an actual template, but after a few cases, I was able to spot the specific point that I wanted. You'll see it in just a moment." June squirted irrigant on the surface of the brain and glanced up at the clock. They had been working for less than an hour after making the skin incision, a good rate of speed. "Doctor White, how are things looking from your standpoint?"

"It's looking like I'm wasting several hours of my life doing work for no pay."

"I was thinking from a patient care point of view, not from a self-serving egotistical point of view."

"What's that supposed to mean?"

June could tell that Andrew's hands had frozen in place, at least until the answer came. "Is the patient stable? Shall we proceed?"

"AS stable as anyone else that's going to be dead in a week."

"That's all I needed to know. Please open the drain and let out fifty CCs of fluid, and let me know when that's done."

She waited, and once the usual amount of time had passed, wondered what was taking so long. "Doctor White?"

"Yes?"

"Fifty CCs?"

"Drained. Shall I close the drain again?"

"Please," June said. "Sheryl?"

"Yes?"

"Please call for Doctor White's attending. He seems to be channeling a great deal of incompetence this evening, and if it doesn't stop soon, his but's going to go flying out the door and you'll be taking over the care of Miss Tavares."

"You can't talk to me that way!" Dr. White griped.

She took a few steps away so she could get a good look at him, dragging the cart with the light source with her. "I wasn't talking to you, Barry. Now, are you man enough to set aside your petty little attitude and do some work?"

"I'll do mine just as well as you do yours."

"Excellent!" June went back to her usual position at the patient's head. "Anybody else have a problem with doing some surgery tonight?"

"Not me," Andrew said cheerfully.

"Me either," Gracie said.

That was enough for June and didn't wait to hear from Sheryl. Taking a pair of pointed scissors in one hand and forceps in the other, she snipped a hole in the tough layer that covered the brain. A slight flood of clear cerebrospinal fluid pulsed out, Andrew sucking it up with his slender suction tip. June continued to cut the dense layer of tissue, opening a window to the pink tissue of the brain. While they worked in tandem, the *beep* of the EKG remained constant and strong.

"So, Sheryl, you haven't had much to say," June prompted. "Sorry to bring you in to work when you had something else better to do."

June saw from the corner of her eye Andrew look at her face. She glanced at him and got a tiny shake of his head back.

"Not that there was much choice," the nurse snarled back.

"What were your plans?"

Andrew let out an audible sigh.

"A fight for justice!"

"Oh, I see," June said after a moment. She'd just stepped in something, and immediately wanted to wipe her feet of it. It appeared Barry had someone on his team. "On a Saturday evening? Don't most people catch a movie or go to a friend's house?"

"This is a very important day for some people," the young Sheryl said in what would be called an 'outside voice' by mothers. "It's called O-Bon, the day we remember our ancestors."

"Yes, that's right," June said. She slid a long, narrow metal blade into the space between folds of brain tissue, followed by another. Attaching them to a spreader, she carefully ratcheted the fold open, millimeter by millimeter. "I was planning to go to the one on Magic Island this evening, until Doctor Lee asked me to help with this surgery."

"That one's for tourists. The real one is on Sand Island, at the channel opening."

"Oh? I guess I didn't hear about that one," June said innocently. Using the light attached to her forehead, she peered down the gap she had made with the retractor. She gave the instrument one more ratcheting click open. "I guess I don't know much about Honolulu yet."

"I thought that festival never got its permit?" Andrew said to the nurse positioned somewhere behind them.

June listened to Andrew as he discussed the unofficial event that was being held illegally. She knew then it was the festival that had stirred up trouble with the city and county, the one she had read about in the newspaper just before the surgery.

"Are you allowed to have something like that if there isn't a permit?" Dr. White asked.

Sheryl postured. "We can if we want!"

June tended to agree with the girl. She wasn't familiar with that park, but if it were large enough to hold the people, why not grant the permit and stay on friendly terms with citizens, instead of antagonize them? By not granting permits to peaceful gatherings, the government often stirred up more trouble when people assembled anyway.

It was time to proceed on to the next phase of the surgery, the microscopic phase. The learning part of the procedure for Andrew was mostly done, the complex approach to the area of the tumor. After talking it out with Andrew, they decided she would do the resection. She would sit in a chair linked to a large microscope that she could move around with her hands and make fine focusing adjustments with foot pedals. It would require several hours of sitting still and tedious work, which she could trade off and share with Andrew, the point of them being there. It would also be the trickiest work they would do all evening.

June had her headlight and loupes removed, and Sheryl helped swing the movable microscope into place. It was a large device, several feet tall, heavy, and difficult to move until it was in position. Settling into the chair and moving the head of the scope around to in front of her, June prepared for the longest part of the surgery: resection of the tumor. That would be done with tiny instruments she would reach through the tunnel, pulling out tiny bits of tumor, one piece at a time. Andrew took up a position just next to her, looking through oculars of his own.

"So, I'm curious why the city didn't grant the permit?" June asked once she had begun working under magnification.

"Because the city hates my family!" Sheryl almost shouted.

That got everyone's attention, their heads bobbing up in unison.

"Okay," June said after a moment.

"No, it's not okay! The city won't let us have our celebration, just like they desecrated our family's graves!"

"The city..." June began to say, still working under magnification.

"The city, the county, the state, they're all in this together! It's a plot to drive my family away!"

"A plot?" Dr. White asked. "Why don't they want you to live here?"

His questions went ignored.

When June paused for a moment, Andrew nudged her. He gave her a look, which she didn't understand, having never worked with him before. Much of the face of workers in the OR was hidden by caps and surgical masks, so most of the facial expressions were through eye movements. She didn't know Andrew well enough to know what he meant with his particular expression.

"How did they desecrate your family's graves, Sheryl?" June asked.

"How? Are you an idiot?"

The anesthesia tech that had been in the room for the last few minutes with Dr. White bolted for the door, Gracie sighed, and Andrew froze in place.

June raised her head, looking up from the oculars of the microscope. "Pardon me?"

"They built this hospital right on top of my Auntie!"

June looked back into her oculars. "That's not my fault. And I'd appreciate an apology."

"For what?" Sheryl demanded.

"For implying I'm an idiot."

"You'll get an apology from me when my family gets their graves restored by this hospital."

June pushed away from the microscope, crossed her arms and stood from her chair. She walked over to where Sheryl was standing and glared her down. Being several inches taller than the nurse helped get the point across. "Seriously, I don't know what the city has to do with this hospital and your family's graves, but right now we have a very serious and difficult surgery to do, and you seem to be doing your best to impede our progress with that." June pointed her finger at the unconscious patient. "If you don't want to provide professional, expert nursing care for that patient, we can find someone else to take your place. Capisce?"

June went back to her spot in the chair and tried settling in again. Just as she adjusted the settings on her microscope again, the door opened.

June glanced over to see who it was. "Yes?" she said sharply.

"Yeah, hi, I'm Maddie. I'm just here to offer a break to Sheryl."

"She needs one."

June watched as Sheryl stumbled through a mini-report on the patient before exiting. As soon as the door was closed behind her, the room heaved a collective sigh of relief.

"What's her problem?" June asked no one in particular as she started working again. She picked part of the tumor out and wiped it on a gauze sponge Andrew was holding.

"She hasn't been here for long," Andrew told her. "But as soon as she got here, she started agitating. Nothing so bad as that, though."

"Did I do something to antagonize her?" June asked. "Because seriously, I'd like to be somewhere else right about now also."

"I think anybody associated with the hospital antagonizes her," Andrew said. "Provocation is never far away with her."

"Doctor, she's got her hooks into all of us once or twice," Gracie said. "She sure doesn't like you, though."

"I got that impression. But if she hates this place so much, why does she work here? Sheryl acts like Kapalama Medical is the Evil Empire, but she draws a paycheck from here. I don't get it." June wiped more tumorous tissue on the gauze sponge.

"Don't ask her about that, either. That really sets her off," Gracie said.

"Yeah, well, back to the task at hand. Maddie, we have some tissue that needs to go to pathology for a quick look," June said, still focused on the microscope oculars. "There is someone here for that, right?"

Five minutes after the nurse made the call, a pathologist was in the room, getting a quick rundown on the patient's history from Andrew.

"The thing is, the tumor is much softer than what it looks on the scans," June said to the pathologist. "It's much more of a gelatinous cyst than an organized tumor. There should be both fluid and capsule there for you to see."

The pathologist left with his small specimen, promising a quick return with results from the frozen sections he was planning. After he left, June went back to work under the scope.

"Does that mean you have a shorter time estimate, Doctor Kato?" Dr. White asked.

"Maybe. A lot of this I can remove with suction. The hard part will be getting the capsule out. It's quite friable, but if I'm careful, I might be able to collapse it upon itself."

"What exactly is the problem? What's so hard about dealing with brain jello?" Dr. White asked.

"The problem is…" June said slowly, concentrating on what her instrument tips were doing deep inside the brain. "…I'm working at the bottom of a tunnel about the size of your little finger. But I'm trying to decompress a semi-liquid tumor the size and consistency of an egg. I can blithely go in and suck out the soft stuff. That's the easy part. What's not so easy it getting the outer capsule out, which is also soft, and only about as thick as that eggshell."

"And…"

"And..." she said to interrupt. "...if I leave that capsule behind, a whole new cyst will form. We'd just be back here in a few years, doing this all over again. Not only that, but with the poor vascularity of the surrounding tissues, chemo works only so well, and with the large area that the capsule is in within the brain, radiation would wipe out large areas of vitally important healthy tissue. So, that means the more tissue I can get out this evening, the less chemo needs to be used, which provides an exponentially better outcome for the patient."

"Doesn't sound so difficult," White said.

"Not really. Not much different than removing snot from a spider web...without tearing the web. What you don't want to hear, Doctor White, is that even though the prognosis is good news for the patient, my original time estimate is still the same. We still have several more hours to go."

June listened to the *bleep bleep* of the EKG monitor for a moment.

"But do you know what might make you happy about my approach to this woman's surgical care, Doctor White?"

"No, what?"

"Removing all of the aberrant tissue now is a much lighter economic burden on the patient, the hospital, and support services later."

A phone rang, Andrew confessing it was his. Maddie answered it. "It's your wife, Doctor Lee." She put the phone up to his ear.

"Honey, what's up? I'm right in the middle of something at the hospital and can't really talk."

After getting prompted to do so, Maddie found a way of putting the call on speaker.

"Are we going to Magic Island this evening? Because if we are, we have to leave soon or we'll be late," Andrew's wife said.

Andrew looked at June. "Beth's family is Chinese, but from San Francisco, still new here in Hawaii. She wants to learn some of the Japanese traditions still practiced here, and going for lantern lighting is part of the project to teach the kids to be poly-ethnic."

"Sounds like a fun way of doing it," June whispered.

While Andrew tried explaining where he was and why he was doing a long unscheduled case on a Saturday evening, June talked with Maddie.

"Everybody here is half this, part that, a little bit of something else," June whispered to Maddie.

"Not me," said the blue-eyed nurse. "I'm just about as flash white as a person can get!"

Andrew got June's attention. "Since you won't be able to go to Magic Island this evening, can my wife float a lantern for you?"

"Don't worry about it."

"It's the least we can do, since I have you tied up in here."

"Well, it would have to be two, I guess. But she'd have to write the names on them for me."

"What are the names?" Andrew's wife asked from the phone.

"Oh. Well, do you know the name Fumito?"

103

"How do you write it?"

"The first character is like for literature, that little four stroke one. The second character is just like for man."

"I know those," Beth said. "What's the other name?"

"My grandmother, Haruno. Just write the character for spring. If you know the old-fashioned way of writing it, that's even better."

"You want their last names? Or a message?"

Already feeling self-conscious for asking the favor, June decided against anything further.

"That should be enough. But she doesn't mind?" June asked.

"No, you're spending your evening with me," Andrew said. "Maybe next year you can come back and join us."

"She seemed nice," June said after the call ended.

"She better be. She can't cook worth a darn."

"Not even Chinese food?"

"Her biggest culinary feat to date is reheating takeout in the microwave."

Her surgical mask hid June's smile. "Ah yes, the plague of the modern bride. Not a single one of us can make anything more complicated than a bowl of noodle soup."

"Making coffee in the morning is too complicated for her. I don't know how she managed to get a PhD in microbiology and a nice job with the state, but she can't boil water to save herself."

"Is she pretty?" June asked.

"Of course!"

"I've seen her," Gracie added. "She's very pretty."

"Well, would you rather have an ugly wife that can cook fine cuisine, or a pretty one you can take to restaurants?" June asked.

"That's not fair!"

Just then, the pathologist returned with the good news that the tissue specimen was not cancerous after all, instead a benign cyst. Just as he was leaving the room, Sheryl returned. For whatever reason, she brought a floor mop with her and leaned it in the corner next to the door.

"Can you stay, Maddie?" Andrew whispered to the nurse that was standing next to him. She had taken up a position to watch the progress of the procedure on a flat screen monitor.

"Gotta go, sorry. Sheryl's the neuro expert anyway. You'll be in good hands."

June sighed, Andrew shifted, and Gracie began to hum quietly to herself. Dr. White acted as the statue, on his stool next to his anesthesia machine, making notes on a clipboard.

"How was your break, Sheryl?" Gracie asked after a moment.

She never got an answer.

"Do you know if someone is coming in to let me out for a break?" Gracie asked her.

Still no answer.

Instead of worrying about them, June took over the task of teaching Andrew a bit more about her approach.

"By using that ratio template tool I taught you earlier, you'll always find the correct location of the sulcus you want, Andrew. Invaluable for third ventricle procedures. Today, however, we won't have to enter the ventricle, since all of the tumor seems to be excluded from it. Which is the best news this woman could get."

June pulled out another gelatinous wad of yellow tissue and wiped it on a gauze pad.

"I could take over, June. You could even leave, if you like, since this is much less complex than what we originally thought, and I've seen your approach."

"Are you sure?" June said, a smile growing on her face behind her mask. Her neck was beginning to tighten from sitting still, leaning forward, peering into the microscope oculars for the last three hours.

"Sure, not a problem at all. I mean, I'm not trying to chase you away, but you might still be able to make it to the festival."

"Well, I've already given that assignment to your wife. I'd hate to make it seem pointless."

"Seriously," he said. "I can give you her phone number and maybe the two of you can meet? She'd like to make a few…"

"She's not going anywhere," Sheryl said from right next to the door.

She grabbed the mop she had brought with her and slid it through the door handles, preventing anyone from coming in. She hurried over to the single door at the opposite side of the room and turned the dead bolt, locking that door also. She then went to stand behind June and Andrew.

"Seriously, Sheryl. You really need to get…" June began to say.

There was an audible click, and June felt the pressure of something hard on the back of her head.

Chapter Nine

"Uh oh," Dr. White muttered from where he sat on the other side of the patient.

"What are you doing, Sheryl?" June tried asking as calmly as she could. As soon as she had heard the click, she knew what it was, the unmistakable metallic sound of a pistol being cocked. She also assumed the firm pressure on the back of her head was the muzzle of the gun.

"Nobody goes anywhere," Sheryl said slowly and carefully.

With her two tiny instruments in her grips, June set her hands in her lap. "Okay."

Sitting stock still, June could see Andrew lean back, finally realizing what was happening right next to him. He began to talk but his voice cracked. He tried speaking again. "June, she's…"

"I know, Andrew. Please just stand still and be quiet," June told him in an even voice, as even as she could make it right then. "Let me manage this, okay?"

"Oh my…" Gracie muttered.

"Doctor Kato, she's holding a gun to the back of your head," Dr. White told her.

"I'm acutely aware of that, Doctor White. I think the who, what, where, when, and how factors of the situation have been satisfied. I'm currently engaged in wondering why."

"Shut up," commanded Sheryl. She reached into June's sterile gown and found the pocket where June had put her phone. Grabbing it, she pulled it free and dropped it in her own pocket.

"Doctor Lee, where's your phone?"

"On the counter by the chart."

Sheryl collected that phone also before going to Dr. White. Aiming her pistol at arm's length at him, she had him set it on the floor and kick it to her.

"Gracie?" she asked. "Put the scalpels in a tray and hand them to me."

The scrub nurse did as she was told. "My phone's in my locker."

Sheryl went back to June, pressing the muzzle against the back of her head again.

"I'm in charge now."

"Yes, you are," June said. "Just one question, though. Am I supposed to do surgery with a gun aimed at my head?"

"You're not supposed to be doing surgery at all. No one should be doing surgery in this operating room."

"Oh? This patient doesn't deserve her operation?" June asked. Her hands were folded in her lap, somewhat hiding her two pointed instruments. What Sheryl hadn't seen though, was that June had cleverly hid a pointed surgical instrument in a fold of fabric in her surgical gown.

"That's not the point. The point is, this operating room shouldn't be here."

"Because?" June asked.

"It is built right on top of the old Mizutani Graveyard."

"And your family was buried there," June summed up. "You told us that earlier."

"Still are buried here. And with this building right on top of them, this operating room in fact. Their gravestones might be gone, but they aren't."

"But Sheryl, surely you must see how holding a gun to my head won't change that. Violence in a situation like this solves nothing."

"Something has to change, and it begins tonight."

"Yes, you're absolutely right. Something needs to change, and it should happen as soon as possible. But we're right in the middle of something here. What if we finish this surgery, and then we can begin the dialogue in a much more congenial way?"

Sheryl whacked June in the back of the head with the gun muzzle, getting a wince from June.

"Don't talk down to me."

"No one's talking down to you," Andrew told her.

"Shut up."

"Andrew, please let me manage this," June pled.

"But…"

"Since the gun is pressed against my head, I think that gives me the right to tell you to shut the hell up and let me manage this. Okay?"

"Sure!"

"Barry, you got any problems with me being spokesperson?"

"I'm good with it."

The muzzle of the pistol squirmed on the back of June's head while Sheryl talked. "Why don't all of you shut up?"

June knew a different tack needed to be followed, but still needed to keep control of the situation. If a gun pressed to the back of her head could be considered control. Most of all, her thoughts didn't need interference right then.

She decided on a bit of levity. "And I thought that when I came here the worst trouble I would find would be a few mosquitoes in the evening." She began to sigh, but it turned into a heave of suppressed emotion.

"You talk too much."

"Probably."

Levity didn't work, so she decided to keep her mouth shut and let someone else try talking sense with Sheryl.

"Sheryl, she has a point," Andrew said with measured care in his tone. "Doctor Kato came here for a conference, and I talked her into doing this case with me. She's just visiting. She's not involved in this issue at all."

June felt the pressure of the muzzle lift from her head.

"We're not done. I might step back, but that doesn't mean I'm leaving. And neither is the gun. I still make the rules in here."

"Can I get back to work?" June asked after a moment.

"If everybody behaves and nobody tries to be a hero, you can work."

June's shoulders slumped. When she picked up the forceps and dissecting instrument she had been using, she couldn't control the slight tremor that had started in her hands.

"Want me to take over, June?" Andrew asked quietly.

"Sheryl, Andrew and I are going to change places, okay?"

She heard the woman take a couple of steps back. She also had been paying attention for any further clicks, indicating that the safety on the gun had been flipped on or the gun uncocked. As far as she could tell, the gun was still ready to be fired with a simple press of the finger.

With all the self-defense training she'd had in her life, even dealing with people with guns, she'd never learned how to disarm someone when they had the gun pressed to the back of her head. The best advice she ever heard about that was to comply with all demands, and survive to the next moment.

June slowly stood from her chair, careful not to make eye contact with the woman holding the gun. Mostly she didn't want to know if it was still aimed at her. Andrew took the place as primary surgeon, sitting in the chair, adjusting the armrests and microscope. June took up her position as assistant, holding only the slender suction tip in her hand, ready to slip it into the channel to dry the area at which Andrew would work.

June had tried to see with her peripheral vision if Sheryl had moved, but couldn't tell. She had to distract herself from the pissed-off person standing somewhere behind her with a gun.

"Doctor White, how is the patient doing?" June asked.

"Railroad track vital signs."

"Are you using nitrous?"

"No, per your request."

She watched as Andrew took out another glob of tumor. "Our worksite is pretty wet. Could you please let fifty milliliters of CSF from her lumbar drain?"

"Okay, done," he said a couple of minutes later.

"It's still clear?"

"Yep."

"Have you checked labs and arterial blood gases lately?"

"A couple hours ago, and they were fine. I thought in the present circumstances, we could suspend with further ones."

"I agree," June muttered while peering through the microscope oculars, watching Andrew work. "She's putting out urine?"

"A hundred cc's per hour."

"Well, we're making good headway here. Andrew is a fast worker. If all goes well, we should be done in two more hours. An hour for tumor and an hour to close."

June felt the nudge of a gun muzzle at the back of her head again.

"That doesn't mean you're going anywhere," Sheryl said.

Holding her head still, June closed her eyes. "I didn't think I was."

Andrew looked at Sheryl. "Why don't you keep me here and let the others go when the time comes?"

Sheryl glared at him. "Go back to work."

Andrew looked through his oculars. "You do realize she's pregnant, right?"

"Well, I guess that's two lives she needs to worry about."

"Thanks for the gesture, Andrew, but let's not stir up more trouble," June said.

They worked in silence for a while, June listening to the steady *beep...beep...beep* of a monitor. June was even developing the hope that once the emotions in the room settled, Sheryl would change her mind. Maybe all she needed was an escape plan handed to her. With that in mind, she began trying to devise a way for the young nurse to find the exit with no one trying to be heroic and chase her down. Just as she was deciding on how to proceed, someone broke the silence.

"As soon as they're done, I have to get this patient to the ICU, Sheryl," Dr. White said. "She can't stay in here indefinitely."

"Fine. You and Doctor Lee will take her there." Sheryl looked at Gracie. "Gracie, you'll be able to take your instruments to the washroom."

June waited for her instructions, and evidently Dr. Lee did also. "What about Doctor Kato?" he asked.

"She stays here with me. And if anyone even thinks about getting clever and tries jumping me, forget it. I'm the one with the gun, not you."

June's spirit sank. There was no cleansing breath or sigh deep enough that could release the tension that built in those few words. While still living in Los Angeles, she had taken up fight training and self-defense as a way of keeping fit. Over the many years of training once a week, she learned many techniques to disarm someone with weapons, including a pistol aimed at her from close range. But it had been a year since she'd trained, she was now pregnant and not nearly as fit. Plus, none of the scenarios she'd practiced had been while being held hostage in an operating room, with a gun pressed to the back of her head.

She had a decision to make. She could resort to violence and try to disarm the nurse, but risk her pregnancy and life. Or an innocent bystander's life. She could wait it out, and try talking sense into an angry—and quite possibly psychotic—women who acted as though she had nothing to lose. Maybe the best thing was the first lesson she'd learned in self-defense, and that was to survive into the next moment.

Dr. Lee tossed down his two instruments. "You can't keep June trapped in here with you!"

June felt the pressure on the back of her head waver a bit.

That forced June into making the hasty decision of keeping dialogue open. "It's okay, Andrew. She can do anything she wants. Sheryl needs her voice to be heard, and if it has come to holding me hostage in the neuro room at Kapalama Medical Center, then that's what we'll do."

"But…"

"Maybe the best thing for you to do is take her message to the administration of the hospital, and tell them how important Sheryl's concerns really are. But we need to finish this surgery first."

The young woman whacked June in the back of the head again. "Don't brown-nose me. I can see through that."

"I'm not. But I also don't feel like getting shot. And if we have to go to these drastic measures for your message to finally get heard, fine. We'll tell the world. I'll do the dance of the seven veils in the middle of Waikiki Beach, if it keeps me alive."

The intercom in the room crackled to life.

"Are you almost done in there?" a woman's voice asked. "If you don't need anything, the rest of us are going home."

"You can go!" Sheryl called out before anyone else could answer.

As quickly as that, the intercom went silent again.

Chapter Ten

Two intense and nearly silent hours later, June sat on a stool in the corner of the room, with Sheryl still aiming her gun at her. The case was done, Dr. Lee wrapping a gauze dressing onto the patient's head.

"Gracie, you can bring in the stretcher. But I'm counting to ten. If you don't have the stretcher here in the room by the time I get to ten, the woman gets it," Sheryl instructed from where she stood. She stood stock still, her arm stretched out to the side, the gun pressed up against June's head. She had an 'I mean business' look to her scowl.

June had no choice but to watch the others move the patient onto the stretcher, hooking up monitoring lines to transport monitors, moving IVs to the stretcher. She and Sheryl had become as one, linked by the muzzle of a pistol.

"What about our phones?" Dr. White asked, just before they rolled out the door.

"I'm keeping them. And I know you're going to call security and the cops as soon as you're out there. Just so you know, if anybody thinks of being heroic by rushing the room, the woman gets it first."

"Are you sure it's worth it?" White asked her, pausing the momentum of the stretcher for a moment. "Going to jail for your cause?"

"I'm willing to join my ancestors, if that's what it takes for our voices to be heard." Sheryl nodded her head in June's direction. "And I'll take others with me."

White shook his head, Andrew pushed the stretcher, and Gracie rushed from the room with her cart of instruments.

As soon as the team was out the door and on their way to the Intensive Care Unit with the patient, Sheryl slid the mop handle through the door handles again.

"So…just the two of us," June said quietly.

"Shut up. You can take your gown and gloves off now."

"I might get cold."

Keeping the gun aimed at June, Sheryl went to a small linen cabinet and grabbed a sheet, tossing it at June. "Wrap up in that."

June stood to take off her surgical gown and rubber gloves.

"And no more tricks. That stunt you tried pulling by hiding the dissector wasn't real smart."

"Neither is holding me hostage."

"Shut up."

"Make me," June chanced saying.

"I could put a bullet through that stupid head of yours. That would make you shut up."

"But doing that loses all your bargaining power. As long as I'm alive and able to speak for your cause, you have power."

"Just shut up, will you?"

June tossed away her surgical garb and wrapped the sheet around her shoulders. "Will you please quit telling me to shut up. You should know by now I'm not going to."

"What're you gonna do? Beat me up?"

"If I have to, I will. And I'm getting real close to it."

"Ha! What a skinny hapai girl gonna do to me, with a gun in my hand?"

June cocked her head and set her gaze on Sheryl's eyes. "Want to find out?"

"You can't get this gun away from me. Nobody could."

"Okay, I'll prove it to you. And I won't even inflict any pain either. Go to the computer, get onto the Internet, and type in K-R-A-V M-A-G-A." The girl stalled, but June nodded at the computer on the counter. "Go ahead, type it in and find the training center at the West Hollenbeck Community Center."

She watched as the girl typed quickly with the gun in one hand.

"So what? Big deal! You know a website. Doesn't mean you know anything about doing that fight stuff."

"Go to the page with the pictures. See the black guy with the bald head? His name is Jukey. He was my teacher for over ten years. Scroll down to the Japanese guy with the USMC T-shirt on. That's Mick, my training partner right up until I moved here."

"What do I care about them?"

"Scroll down to the woman in the black T-shirt with the rainbow peace sign on it. She has headgear and sparring gloves on. Does she look familiar?"

"That's you?"

"A few years ago when I still had long hair. Scroll down a little more. Now what do you see?"

"You're wrestling with that Marine guy on the floor?"

"You can't tell from the picture, but he's tapping out right there."

"How'd you do that?"

"I was feeling pre-menstrual that day." June grinned at her captor. "Now I have a baby to protect. And you better frickin' believe I'm going to protect it."

Sheryl logged off the computer.

"You want me to end this? Because I'm not going to."

"I don't expect you to," June told her, now believing she was able to get the girl to settle some. "Right now, I expect you to keep being stupid until you make a massive mistake. Then I get the gun, and you get the crap beat out of you. And you know what? After you calling me stupid half a dozen times, and telling me to shut up, I kinda feel like it."

Sheryl took half a step back. "What do you want from me, then?"

"For starters, I want you to stop aiming that gun at my baby."

They stared at each other for a moment, the gun still aimed generally at June's body.

"I really doubt you want to shoot me. But I'm a bit concerned a mistake might happen and the gun would go off accidently."

"Yeah, right. And as soon as I put the gun in my pocket, you attack. I don't think so."

"Seriously Sheryl, I don't need you to put the gun away for me to go on the offensive. By the time I'm done speaking this sentence, I could have the gun out of your hand and you disabled..." June nodded her head. "...permanently."

"Hapai girl...you can do that pregnant?"

"My baby just gives me one more reason to."

The room phone rang. June tried to listen in on the brief conversation Sheryl had. The gist of it was that no one was coming in, no one was going out, and a phone call would follow later on the specification of terms.

'Great,' June thought. 'I get to spend the remainder of the evening negotiating my own release.'

"Now what?" June asked.

"I don't know. I've never done this before."

"Maybe we should sit down and talk for a while. Calmly."

"Any tricks and I shoot."

"I'm too tired for tricks."

"Fine." Sheryl waved June to one corner of the room, indicating she should sit on the floor.

"Could I sit on one of the pads from the bed?"

Sheryl aimed her gun again. "Say please."

June stared her down. "Forget it. I'm doing nothing nice to you until I get an apology. But as your hostage, you better start treating me a whole lot nicer, if you want your pathetic negotiations to go anywhere."

Sheryl tossed one of the thin pads from the bed, June settling on it. She reached forward and rolled the stool to in front of her, propping her legs on the top before leaning back against the wall. Her legs had swollen more than ever from standing so long during the long surgery.

June did her best to completely ignore the fact there was a gun in the room with her. Sheryl remained standing, the gun still in her hand, no longer pointed at June, but at the floor somewhere in front of her.

She slid up the thin pant legs of the pajama-like surgical garb and looked at her ankles. She pressed a thumb into the puffy area around the knucklebones.

"I must have ten gallons of water in my legs," June muttered.

"You okay?" Sheryl asked.

"Yeah, fine. It's just that when I haven't been sitting absolutely still doing that long surgery, I've been standing. I've been on my feet all day long. If I don't get my feet up a couple of times each day, they balloon up. As soon as these things drain, I'm going to have the fullest bladder in town." June flicked the pants legs down again. "Which reminds me…"

"Forget it. You're not going shi-shi or nothing else."

"Can I at least take my head cover off?"

Sheryl gave June a nod of acceptance. June pulled the loose cover off, inspected it and set it aside. She ran her fingers through her hair a few times, tried fluffing it, then tried tucking as much as she could behind her ears. What had been an ultra-chic style a few months before had grown to her eyebrows and covered her ears. When she got home, she needed to get a haircut. If she got out of this jam.

Sheryl spoke up, but in a quieter voice. "You liked your highlights?"

June was surprised at the question. She pinched a lock of it in her fingers and held it out to look at it cross-eyed. "Yeah, I did. Several months old now though. My hair was so short then, cute, but the color made it more feminine."

"Would you do it again? Color takes so long to grow out."

"Not while I'm pregnant, or breastfeeding. Just concerned about the chemicals, you know?" June muttered, running her hand over her tummy again. It was quickly becoming a habit, to gently caress her belly whenever she thought of the baby. June knew that a bridge of some sort was forming, and decided to take a tentative step onto it. "I can't see your hair. Do you have highlights?"

Sheryl pulled her cap off also, rubbing her head. There was a slash of magenta along one temple, the rest of her hair in ear-covering loose layers. June saw the wave in it, the body it created, and was jealous for a moment.

"Is it naturally wavy?"

"Yep. But enough of the girltalk."

"Why?" June asked.

"It's boring."

They sat quietly for a few minutes. As the time passed, June could sense the tension subsiding a bit. She looked over at Sheryl, now seated on a stool across the room, the gun stationed in her lap. Their eyes met, and June offered a polite smile.

"Sheryl, just exactly what is this all about? Am I supposed to find some magical way of lifting up the hospital and moving it a few feet to one side?"

"I know that's impossible."

"You don't seriously expect them to tear down the hospital, do you? This is a new facility, and one of the nicest I've even seen. They have state of the art equipment, and talented people working here. They won't even consider building a replacement, just because it's been parked on top of an old graveyard."

"Why not?"

June did her best to not roll her eyes. "First, tell me what happened a few years ago before they started building. How did they ever get the permits to build on this site, if there was a graveyard here? City governments usually won't do that, will they?"

"They didn't. It wasn't an official cemetery, but just a place to bury dead family members years ago. There are many such graveyards in the islands." Sheryl looked almost as if she were going to cry. "There was a great tragedy with leprosy in the past and many people suffered. Maybe you know about the disease, maybe not. But the people didn't die from that disease, but usually from another infection."

"I thought the state or the territory, whatever government was in charge in those days, collected the people and took them to another island to live?" June asked.

"They did, to Molokai. Because they didn't understand the disease back then. That was half the heartbreak, when families were torn apart because the sick were carted off, almost kidnapped by the government officials. Healthy babies were taken away from afflicted parents. That little town on Molokai is still there, still with a few of those people, but instead of calling it a colony, it's been turned into a national park."

"I see. But what do they have to do with your family's graveyard, the graveyard that used to be here?"

"It was known as the Mizutani Graveyard. You won't find it on any map. It wasn't named after a person, but just given that name because of the area."

"Watery Valley?" June asked, translating the Japanese name into English.

"For the little streams that come down from the pali. In the past, there was a little stream that flowed closer to here, just past the edge of the graveyard. But it got rerouted at some point, probably when houses were built."

"I guess I still don't understand why you're so upset. This all seems so very personal to you," June said to the girl. Sheryl was no longer agitated, but more reflective, subdued.

"It's personal because…" Sheryl sounded agitated again, but settled herself after a moment. "My Auntie…actually, my father's auntie is buried here. She had the disease."

"That's sad. She wasn't taken away?"

"The family hid her. She got the disease as a young woman. She didn't want to leave the island, her whole ohana was here on Oahu. Instead, she came to her brother's house, where they let her live her life. She

127

never went out, only late at night when she knew she could be alone and not be seen by neighbors. When she first moved in with the family, they made all sorts of excuses about her, she was frail, sickly, didn't like going out in public, those sorts of things. After a while, the neighbors forgot about her, and nobody ever came looking for her. My father was a small boy when she finally died."

"And they buried her in the Mizutani Graveyard?" June asked quietly.

"It was supposed to be a secret graveyard, a place for lepers and the mentally ill. Right from the very beginning, everybody in the neighborhood knew it was there. But island people being so superstitious, nobody would ever go there, except to bury someone. Even the kids, as curious as they can be sometimes, never went."

"So, Mizutani was basically a secret graveyard reserved for lepers and mentally ill, a place that no official ever knew about until only recently? But I thought there were headstones, and they had been moved to somewhere else?"

"That's the sad thing. There were headstones, of sorts. A family would go up to the pali, find a flat rock, bring it home. Lava rocks are too hard to chisel a name, so names were painted on the surface of the rock. Once the rock was put in place, it didn't take long for vines and roots to cover it."

"And you saw these?"

"Once when I was a kid, my dad brought me to visit the place. We found rocks with paint, but time and weather had washed most of the paint from the rocks. We never did find Auntie Maile's."

"Her name was Maile? That's a fairly common Hawaiian name, isn't it? I thought you said she was Japanese?"

"Quite common. Her real name was Mari. But when she moved in with my grandfather's family, they started calling her Maile, maybe to help hide her identity. Just like everybody here back then, she was dark-skinned. If someone had happened to meet her when she went out late at night, they'd just assume she was some part Hawaiian." Sheryl looked down at the gun in her lap. "But she never really went out much…until she died."

"That's sad. I didn't know all that went on here, that there was that much leprosy."

"Thousands in the old days. Every little neighborhood suffered a few victims."

"And your grandfather and Auntie Maile lived near here?"

"In a little house, just the next street down, around the corner. It's a bed and breakfast for tourists now. Not that they care about the history of the place."

June thought of the name of the place she was staying, Auntie Maile's B and B. Only a block away, it had to be the same house of Sheryl's ancestor; it would be too much coincidence if it wasn't. Then she remembered the scrapbook she had looked through the night before, at the pictures of the house throughout the decades. "I'm sure they do."

Sheryl laughed for a moment. "I bet if they knew a leper had lived in that house, those tourists wouldn't stay there!"

"Probably not."

Chapter Eleven

"And that's what happened. It was reported in the newspaper one day, once construction had begun. When the bulldozers began clearing away the trees to level the area, someone noticed painting on a few of the rocks. Most of the writing was in Chinese or Japanese characters, some were Hawaiian words. Curious, one guy asked some of the old people in the neighborhood what they were. At first, no one talked. Then he found someone who explained what they were."

"What happened then?"

"That guy, I suppose he thought he was being nice. He came back at night a few times and went looking for rocks with paint on them. What I heard was that when he found one, he'd put it in the back of his pickup. When he had a few, he took them up to the old Chinese cemetery at the top of the valley. He didn't know what else to do with them, so he put them in the back corner where no one might notice. I guess he quit looking when he couldn't find anymore, or maybe when they starting digging the hole to build the building."

"Seems very kind that he would do such a thing, and on his own time. Like he wanted to preserve them somehow. But when they dug, they never found the graves?"

"Nobody ever said anything. It was a construction company from the mainland. Maybe they found bones, maybe not. If they did, they probably just kept working, not wanting to stir up trouble or delay the construction. If it had been a local company, they would've halted work if they found a bone."

It really was sad, the old graves being disturbed like that. Not much could be done now, though. June gave it some thought, about how to proceed, if Sheryl was open to suggestions yet. "Isn't there a way you could arrange them in that cemetery somehow?"

They were sitting together now, only a few feet apart. June was hungry, but even more, she needed to go to the bathroom. But asking for permission wasn't worth the risk of getting Sheryl riled up again. They had been talking for a couple hours, and except for a few dramatically shed tears by Sheryl, it had been mostly calm.

"They're not buried up there. Those people are buried here, right here underneath this building, right about where this operating room is."

"Does it make that much difference? It would be a place for people to go visit the memory of them. That's all a cemetery really is, a place set aside for someone to visit their ancestors."

"What about your family? Are your grandparents still alive?" Sheryl asked June.

It was June's turn to stare down into her lap. Her fingers had been wrestling with each other, but she willed them to stop. "My grandparents died over twenty years ago, when I was in college."

"Where are they buried?"

"Oh, they were cremated. After, we got together as a family, the five of us the first time. Mom, Dad, me and my sister, Grandma. We took Granddad's ashes up into the hills near their old home and sprinkled them into the sky on a windy day." June remembered the scene vividly. It was in the hills not far from her old home in Los Angeles, at a small pond she would run past occasionally. "It was something, watching the ash swirl in the sky. Around and around it went, like it didn't want to leave us, until the sky drew it up and away. As we walked back to the house, Grandma said she wanted the exact same thing when it came to her time."

"And did you guys?"

June pursed her lips and blew away the urge to cry. "Only a few months later. The exact same place, again on a windy day. But the Santa Ana winds were especially strong that day, and Grandma went with one big whoosh."

"She must've missed her husband, and wanted to get back to him as quickly as possible."

"That's a nice way of looking at it." June looked at Sheryl in a new light. She really was caring and sensitive. If it weren't for the gun in her lap and being held hostage in a cold operating room with a full bladder, she could be likeable. "But you know Sheryl, holding me hostage isn't going to change anything. It's only making things worse for you."

"I have to do what I can. And if I have to do this to make my voice heard, then that's what I'll do. The city didn't grant us the permit to hold a lantern lighting

133

festival at Sand Island. I guess that made me sorta desperate."

"What are you expecting from the hospital?"

"I want them to make it right."

"Come on, Sheryl. You're educated. You have to ask for something specific, and something realistic."

"I want Auntie, and all the others, to have a real cemetery, not just be in a pile of rocks where they don't belong."

"Okay, that's good. That's two things we can request. That the headstones are in a real cemetery, and that they're closer to here."

"I want them here!"

"Okay, here."

June had gone for the walk in the neighborhood the night before. All she really saw was the street to the little grocery store, and the meditation center. One idea she had off the top of her head was the little park next to the meditation center. She needed to proceed carefully. But she was turning herself into an ally now, and didn't want to botch that by letting on she was staying at the bed and breakfast where her auntie had lived, and ultimately died in.

"Is there a place near here that isn't being used for something else? A park or a green spot near the stream you mentioned?"

"There's a couple places, I suppose. But it wouldn't be the same. Maybe it would make the living happy, but what about the spirits? They must be wandering these days."

"Maybe so. I didn't see much of the area around the building before I came in this morning."

"The whole place is surrounded by parking lots, walkways, driveways, and the parking garage."

"There isn't any kind of employee sitting area outside?" June asked.

"Only one of those smoker's tents," Sheryl muttered. "It's not very big, and they'd never give it up. That's out in the middle of the employee parking lot anyway."

"How many stones are we talking about?" June asked. "I'm trying to figure out how much space is needed."

"What I remember of the little graveyard was only about twenty feet by thirty feet."

"A little courtyard with a memorial garden would be nice. Would it be okay if visitors were able to sit there for a while? Sometimes people like to do that," June offered.

"There's a little chapel inside the hospital for that."

"It could be similar, but outdoors, with benches. Maybe have some little palms, a few ferns, some of those ti plants. Those are supposed to be sacred, right?"

"Yeah."

June knew exactly where there was a space just the right size, and it was already decorated similar to what she had described. At each side of the main entrance to the hospital were two large garden spaces, separating the entrance from the main parking lot. It already had a few palms and large ti plants, and a variety of other tropicals growing cheerfully in the sun. It wouldn't take much to put in a little path, arrange the stones, and have a decorative lantern nearby. But she wanted Sheryl to think of it on her own. "There must be someplace around the building."

"I don't know. There's nothing."

Maybe Sheryl never went in the front door, but only used the side doors directly from the employee parking lot. "I noticed there were plantings in front of the hospital near the main entrance when I came in this morning. I wonder if the hospital would allow that area to be used?" June finally prompted.

"Oh yeah! It's big enough, and close."

"And people could see it. There could be a little memorial plaque of some sort telling the story, that bit of history of the neighborhood. Would something like that work?"

"I'd like that," Sheryl said with her first smile of the night.

"It'd have to be discrete. I mean, hospitals generally don't like the idea of graveyards being at the front door. But otherwise, would it work? Would you drop the lawsuit and end all this…" June swung her hand in the air, in front of them. "…whatever this is?"

Sheryl looked at June for a moment. "If the hospital agrees."

Chapter Twelve

The intercom crackled to life, the hourly check from the police that started early in the night. Throughout the night, June occasionally saw the reflection of someone out in the hall on the window glass. She had assumed it was police, massing in the hallway, ready to make a strike if necessary. Mostly, they remained hidden from view, and made their hourly calls on the intercom, as agreed upon by Sheryl.

"We're fine!" June called out. "If you could get a hospital administrator to call into the room, it would be great!"

"Think they'll go for it?" Sheryl asked once the intercom flipped off.

"You have to try. It's a lot better than a lawsuit and some big drawn-out ordeal in the media." June tried smiling, but her bladder was aching something fierce. "But you know, they'll spin this their way, to make it look like they were the ones who thought of it, just so they can come out of the deal looking good."

"I know."

Sheryl began to fiddle with the gun in her lap again, June watching. She never had uncocked it, or put the safety on. One wrong tap of the trigger, and something or someone was coming away with a large hole.

"The police won't be happy, either."

"Oh, they're not gonna be happy at all! I knew that coming into this. But I had to get my point across."

"You'll have to go to jail, at least for a while until this all gets straightened out."

Sheryl looked down at the gun in her hand, turned it over and looked at the other side. She touched the trigger, feeling it with the tip of her finger. Watching the girl, June realized what had been in Sheryl's mind all along, that if anyone would've been shot that night, it would've been self-inflicted.

"I know," Sheryl mewed. "Better than the alternative, I guess."

"I suppose so."

The room phone rang.

"There's the administrator we asked for," June said quietly. "You should talk to them."

The phone rang again, but Sheryl sat still.

"Just tell them what we talked about, how everything would be settled if there was a little memorial garden at the front of the hospital."

The phone rang a third, then fourth time.

"Yeah."

Sheryl turned the gun over in her lap when the phone rang a fifth time.

"Are you going to talk to them?" June asked quietly, hoping it sounded encouraging.

Sheryl held the gun up at arm's length, almost admiring it.

The phone rang.

"Sheryl?"

Sheryl stood, and turned. She looked down at where June sat on a pad from the bed, wrapped in the thin sheet.

"May as well get this over with."

June didn't know what to expect next. Something had changed suddenly. She began to fear the worst again, that Sheryl was finally going to turn the gun on herself, or her. But she was too far from Sheryl to try a defensive kick. Perched on the floor leaned back against the wall, she was a sitting duck with nowhere to hide.

The phone had stopped ringing. June waited through endless moments, watching the young woman, wondering what was coming. Sheryl's hand had a tremor in it then, maybe her nerves finally cracking.

The phone never rang again.

"I guess I missed my chance."

"I doubt they'll call back, Sheryl." June couldn't take her eyes off the gun. "You know what would really help you when the police come in here?"

"The police? In here?" Sheryl looked genuinely startled by the idea.

"Yeah. Sooner or later, they'll rush the room. Count on it."

"What'll they do?"

"They'll probably tase and subdue you. They'll shoot you if necessary. Whatever they do, it won't be polite."

Now she looked confused. And exhausted. Her shoulders slumped. The air seemed to go out of her. She lowered the gun to her side, her finger still touching the trigger, her hand shaking. "Why?"

139

"You've held a pregnant woman hostage in here all night. Police don't like that sort of thing."

"Yeah."

"One thing that would really help you is if you weren't holding that gun when they came in. If you unloaded it and set it aside, and we put our hands up, they'd be a lot less aggressive."

Sheryl looked at the pistol again. "I don't know how to use it. I took it out of my brother's room right before I came to work."

"Would you give it to me? I mean, do you trust me, that I won't use it on you?"

"I guess. Maybe they don't know I have it?"

"Oh, I think the others have mentioned it already. Doctor Lee and the others saw it, remember? That's why they haven't come crashing in here earlier." June was feeling pity for her now that Sheryl had got into trouble way over her head. There was no way out, except in shackles. "If we were outside, and no one had seen all this take place, I would've been happy to just throw the gun away and forget all about it. But that can't happen with the way things are."

"We can't hide it?"

"In an operating room?" June asked. "They'd find it. They know it's here."

The phone began ringing again.

"You need to talk to them, Sheryl."

It rang again, and seemed even louder, more insistent than ever.

"End this your way, Sheryl, or they will."

Sheryl started for the phone.

"But give me the gun first."

June reached up and Sheryl gently put the gun in June's hand before turning back to the ringing phone.

As June listened to Sheryl talk on the phone, she uncocked the pistol and removed the magazine of bullets. Next, she ejected the bullet that was in the breach, dropping the bullet into her pocket. Setting the empty gun aside, she removed each bullet from the magazine and set those aside also. Completely empty of ammunition, the gun was finally safe.

June had half-expected the police to come crashing through one of the doors as soon as Sheryl was on the phone. They hadn't. Instead, it gave her time to find a place to toss the bullets she held in her hand. Standing from her spot on the floor and tossing her sheet away, her legs and back were stiff, but she had a chore to do.

She dug through the trashcan next to the anesthesia machine, remembering something Dr. White had tossed in there many hours before. She found the brown plastic bottle that held the liquid anesthesia, what he had replenished his machine with at the beginning of the surgery. It would be perfect for hiding and disposing the bullets.

First, there was something else she had to do, and she needed to act quickly. Listening to Sheryl on her phone call, it sounded like they might finish talking soon.

She grabbed a sheet of paper from the trash. Tearing pieces from it, she wrapped each bullet, and dropped them into the brown opaque plastic bottle one at a time. Once she had them all in there, she screwed the cap back on and shoved the bottle back down into the trash again. Just as she was walking back to where she left the pistol, Sheryl ended her call.

"Good news!" Sheryl said.

"Oh?" June said, bending down to pick up the empty pistol and magazine.

Just then, the racket of a power saw started up outside the double doors. They both spun and watched what was happening. A long blade came through the gap between the doors, cutting through the metal mop handle.

"They're coming in now, Sheryl. But listen. There were no bullets in the gun. Make sure you tell them you knew there were no bullets in the gun, okay? There will be a lot less trouble for you that way!"

The saw was halfway through the metal mop handle. The phone began to ring again.

"But…"

"Never mind everything else. Just tell them you knew there were no bullets in the gun, that you were never going to hurt anyone."

June could see the saw was almost through the mop handle.

"Put your hands in the air, Sheryl. Just give up now and maybe they won't hurt you," June prompted. "And for crying out loud, tell them you gave me the gun, and you knew it was empty."

Pinching the gun between her fingers in one hand and the empty magazine in the other, June raised her hands over her head.

The saw fell through the gap and the two sides of the mop fell away. The double doors burst open, three SWAT officers dressed in black overalls rushing in. All three had weapons aimed at the two women. The second officer held something June recognized as a taser. He swung it back and forth between them.

"Don't tase us!" June said loudly. "I'm pregnant and she surrenders!"

The taser's aim went back and forth, from June to Sheryl, back to June.

June wiggled the gun pinched between her fingers to get their attention. "The gun is empty, the magazine is out. No bullets."

The officer in back went to June and snatched the gun and magazine from her hands. He pushed her toward the wall, and June assumed the position to be searched.

"What's your name?" he asked while patting her down.

"Doctor June Kato."

"You don't want her!" Sheryl screamed. "Don't hurt her!"

After a quick pat-down, the officer called, "Clear!"

The officer kept his hand on her shoulder, holding her in place against the wall. June heard the noise of a scuffle followed by a loud thump, and knew Sheryl was getting taken down by the other two officers.

"Don't resist, Sheryl," June said as calmly as she could. "Just let them put the cuffs on you."

The scuffling noises continued until June heard a whack and a loud grunt, a moan that sounded as if it belonged to Sheryl. Orders were shouted at Sheryl by the men to quit resisting. There was some swearing, street-grade name calling. More heavy footsteps rushed in and June heard the police struggle with getting Sheryl out the door. June was glad she didn't have to watch.

Once the noise settled, the SWAT cop that had June against the wall relaxed and let her step back.

With the new arrival of more officers in the room came a paramedic. He immediately went to June, checking her over. She waved him off, more annoyed at being touched than anything.

"You're okay, though?" the paramedic asked June.

"I'm fine. Nothing happened. But you have no idea of how badly I have to use the toilet."

She grabbed a sheet from the bed and wrapped herself around the waist with it before rushing off to the locker room. Once she was done, police officers were waiting for her.

"We need to talk."

Chapter Thirteen

Talking with officers and detectives took another two hours, just going through the story over and over again. A hospital administrator had shown up to hear Sheryl's demands, delivered via June. She sensed some sort of agreement could be had, if there was more dialogue and in better surroundings than an operating room full of cops

Once she had given her statement to the police, June was allowed to change into the same clothes she had worn into the place the day before. She packed the few things she had brought with her, except her phone. That was still in Sheryl's pocket along with Dr. Lee's and Dr. White's phones when she was arrested. Wondering if she'd ever see it again, she went out to the main lobby where a news conference was already being held.

Darting off in another direction to avoid the ad hoc media event, she saw the corridor that led to the Intensive Care unit and went there. Once she found her patient from the night before, she checked over her neurologic and vital signs, and checked the chart for her progress during the night. The orders that Dr. Lee had written were exactly what she would've given. He really had paid attention to her lecture at the conference the day before.

When she went back down the corridor to leave the hospital, she saw a small group of police investigators. She went directly to the one that had taken her statement earlier.

"Is there any way I can get my phone back?" she asked impatiently. "My whole life in on that phone."

He held out two phones. Taking hers, she assumed the other was either Lee's or White's.

"Do you need a ride anywhere?" he asked politely.

"I'm staying nearby. Thanks, though."

"Pretty big ordeal. You sure you don't want to spend some time with the department psychiatrist to debrief a little?"

"I'm fine, really I am. Just tired. I have a flight home later this morning anyway." She glanced around the area a moment. "Are the others around? Doctor Lee and the others?"

He looked at the small pad of paper in his hand, reading notes. "The young woman's husband came to pick her up a few minutes ago. Doctor White went home early last night."

"I should've figured. What about Doctor Lee?"

"I just got through talking with him. I think he's waiting outside for you."

June went to the front entrance, following a roundabout way to get there to avoid the news conference that was just breaking up. As soon as she was outside, she saw him still dressed in his scrubs. A woman was sitting with him on a bench.

He stood when June got close. "Honey, this is June Kato. She's the one you talked to on the phone last evening."

June shook hands with Mrs. Lee, unable to remember if she had heard the woman's name earlier. "Thanks for going to Magic Island for me."

"It was nothing. But oh my! What a terrible experience!"

June didn't want to talk about, or even think of the long night. She offered a couple of obvious placations, complained of being tired, and reminded herself of the flight she needed to catch later in the morning. She got a brief report from Dr. Lee on the patient's status before they reassured each other they would like to work together again sometime.

"Just under different circumstances," June said, still trying to boost her morale.

"My wife can drop you somewhere if you like?" Lee offered. His wife nodded her head encouragingly.

"My room is just the next block over. It'll be nice just to get the fresh air. But thanks."

They said their farewells, more of an apology from Dr. Lee than anything else.

June was more tired than she let on, and hungry for a change. The early morning sun felt good on her face as she watched the Lees retreat into the building.

There was no reason for June to go back into the hospital. The patient was in Dr. Lee's care, and she knew he could manage her case without her help. Instead, June went to a bus stop nearby and sat. Getting her phone out, she saw dozens of messages waiting for her. She read a few, and ignored the rest.

"Hi Mom. How's Dad with the addition? Is he getting something done?"

She held the phone away from her ear while her mother squawked back. It was exactly as she feared, that the hostage situation had made the news last evening, and her mother and father had stayed up all night waiting for word.

"I got out a few minutes ago. I just need to walk back to the B and B, pack my things, and go to the airport."

After several promises to explain everything when she got home, she begged off. Just as she was about to walk away, someone called to her from behind.

"Doctor Kato?" a man said trotting up to her from the direction of the main entrance. Dark-skinned and haired, he was clad in an aloha shirt of subdued colors and khaki pants.

"Yes?"

"My name is Keane McCullough, one of the administrators here at Kapalama Medical."

"The one Sheryl talked to?"

"That's right."

June just didn't have the patience for more talk right then, especially from an administrator. "I talked with another administrator earlier. But right now I have a plane to catch. So, if you don't mind…"

"I'd like to thank you for what you did," he said to interrupt.

"For doing the surgery or handling Sheryl?"

"Both, I suppose."

He turned her back toward the entrance.

"So, you understand what she wants, right?" June asked him.

"Yes. Apparently, there are some rocks that she wants made into a little rock garden here on the rounds? And if we do that, she'll drop the lawsuit against us?"

"And I think that little foundation of hers would also go away." They got to the front entryway and June stopped, pointing at the small garden areas to each side of the door. "This is where she was thinking the memorial garden could go. Maybe a little stepping stone path, a stone lantern of some sort, and the rocks themselves. It sounds like there's only a dozen or so of them."

"I can't guarantee anything, especially under the circumstances."

"Did you promise anything on the phone?"

"I told her something would be done. But you must understand, it was only to end the situation. We needed to get you out of there, and start a new day."

"And you need to understand there was never much of a situation to begin with. All that girl ever wanted was for Kapalama Medical Center to listen to her. If you would've listened earlier, none of this ever would've happened."

"We had no idea anything was here before we built. From all the records we collected on land usage and property ownership, nothing was here. We never knew anything about painted rocks or graves or lepers until just a few months ago, when she brought the suit

149

against the hospital. We're still trying to locate exactly who it was that moved the rocks, but the general contractor that worked with us back then doesn't know who it was. It's just that somehow a pile of rocks was moved from here to that Chinese cemetery at the end of the valley, and no one knows how they got there. Even Sheryl doesn't know who did it, just the rumor she heard about it."

"I don't know, Mister McCullough. I'm too tired right now to figure out any of it." She couldn't smile, not even a fake one. "It really isn't my problem anymore. But I seriously hope you follow through on any promises you made to the woman, for her sake if not for the hospital's." June turned to walk away, but stopped and looked back at the administrator. "I'm more on her side in this than I am on yours."

Chapter Fourteen

It was still early morning as June walked the short distance back to the bed and breakfast. Few cars plied the quiet residential streets, and no one else was out walking. She went to the little corner grocery store hoping it was open. She needed something to eat, and was reluctant to eat with the people at the inn, if they were even up yet. She wasn't sure of what had been reported on the news, if her name had been revealed as the hospital hostage, but if it had, she would be quizzed endlessly by the strangers at the inn. Right then, she only wanted to put it out of her mind as quickly as possible.

The little store was closed. Reluctant to go back to the inn, June walked across the street to the park next to the meditation center. Someone was seated there. She sat anyway.

"Mind if I join you?"

"In what?" the woman said. She looked familiar.

"Just to sit for a while." June looked at the woman's face, trying to figure where she'd seen her before. "Are you the lady I talked with the other night?"

The old woman replied in Japanese. "You had a long, hard night."

June sighed. "You have no idea."

The old lady chuckled pleasantly.

151

They sat quietly for a few minutes, June daydreaming, listening to the creek gurgle at the other end of the open space. A small group of iridescent green birds flew from a tree and settled onto the ground, pecking through the grass comically.

"Did everything turn out okay?" the old lady asked.

"With?"

"At the hospital?"

"I guess I told you about the conference the other night. It went fine. Seems so long ago now."

"And the rest?"

"Oh, you heard about what happened last night in the operating room? Is it really a big deal on the news?" June asked.

"That part doesn't matter. But it turned out okay, about the rocks?"

"Well, the girl had to go to jail. But it looks like she's going to get the little cemetery she wanted. They'll put in a small memorial garden at the front of the hospital, using the original rocks that were..." June looked at the woman, who was barely paying attention to her. "How did you know about the rocks?"

"Those rocks have been here for a long time, and so have I."

That's when it hit June, who the woman was. The Japanese language, the old-fashioned clothes, the disappearing act on the first evening, firsthand knowledge of the neighborhood. June expected a shiver to sweep through her, but it never came.

"You're Auntie Maile, aren't you? Or do you want to be called Mari?"

The old woman turned her head to look at June again, a shy smile across her lips. Her eyes were dark and wet, tired or maybe it was sadness of missed ages. The wrinkles in her face deepened when she smiled even more.

"It doesn't matter, does it?" she asked quietly.

"No, I suppose not," June said.

She went back to starting her day in the sunshine, watching as one bird encroached closer, pecking at the ground, hopping along the grass playfully.

"Thank you for helping," the old woman said softly.

The bird flitted away. June turned to smile at the woman, but she was gone.

Chapter Fifteen

June was exhausted by the time she got back to her room at Auntie Maile's Bed and Breakfast. It took only a few minutes to shower and change into travel clothes for her trip home. The rest of her things got crammed into her overnight bag. She dug out a business card from her wallet. Just as she was about to call Ken Takahashi, the taxi driver, her phone rang.

She had been waiting for her sister to call. "Hi Amy. What's up?"

"What's up? You were held hostage! Are you okay?"

"I'm fine. Don't listen to Mom's dramatics."

"It's on the LA news!"

"They're probably just blowing it up out of proportion."

"Were you a hostage or not? Held at gunpoint?"

"I guess."

"How can that not be a big deal? And what were you doing in an OR late at night? You went there for a conference!"

"I got roped into doing a tumor case with a surgeon I met at the conference. Then later…Never mind. I'll explain later after some sleep."

She hung up on her sister, mainly because explanations could take hours, if not days. She wasn't up to a scolding right then. All she wanted was to get to the airport and wait in a coffee shop for her plane.

***

"Howzit!" Ken said cheerfully as June climbed in the back of his taxi. "Going home already?"

"Yep, the weekend is done. Time to go home."

"Big kine deal at the hospital last night."

"So I've heard," June said to him. She took up a position to look at the scenery out the window.

Ken chatted on for a few minutes about the hostage news story at the hospital, June barely listening. As she suspected, the news reporters had dramatized much of the story, and maybe Ken was editing a few of the details for effect. Just as he was turning onto a busier boulevard, something occurred to her. She never had gone to Magic Island. It was too late now to float a lantern, but it didn't mean she couldn't at least see the place.

"Ken, are we anywhere near Magic Island?"

"Back other side," he said, tossing his thumb over his shoulder. "You never went?"

"Never got the chance."

"Fun time. Lotsa people there last night. After you mentioned it, I thought I'd take my wife there. Hadn't floated lanterns in ages."

"I'm glad you went."

"Have a good time in Honolulu anyway?" Ken asked.

"A good time?" June's mind almost burned with fatigue, having been up for almost thirty hours by then. She thought of her evening walk the first day she was there, and of meeting Doctors Lee and White at the conference. The old woman at the park flashed through her mind, only a glimmer of a memory. The good news of the patient's new prognosis was almost lost in the shuddering memory of spending the night talking Sheryl out of doing something drastic, life changing. What hit her most profoundly was that she was able to talk a maniac out of using a gun instead of resorting to physical violence. Not that she ever wanted to do it again. "I met a few new people, so yeah, I guess I had a good time."

Ken brought the car to a stop at the airport interisland departures terminal.

"Coming back to see us again?" Ken asked as June paid the fare.

"Someday. But next time, I'll stay in a hotel."

Chapter Sixteen

Justice moved slowly for Sheryl in the following weeks. June had almost forgotten about the affair in the OR with Sheryl and the others, until she was contacted by the Honolulu District Attorney's office to give formal testimony on the case built against the nurse. They called her in, June taking the day off from work to fly to Oahu for the hearing a month later.

With no baggage for the day trip from Maui, she called the taxi driver Ken as soon as she landed in Honolulu. Learning he was at his usual place at the airport, she met him there.

"Came back already!" he said as soon as she was settled in the back seat. "Where to?"

"County courthouse, wherever that is."

When they got there, she gave him some cash.

"Ken, I just need to give a quick deposition. Can you come back in about an hour?"

Ken decided to wait, and not charge her for it. No other fares had come along while June was in the courthouse, and she found him waiting at the curb when she was done.

"Back to airport?"

She checked for messages and looked at the time on her phone. "Kapalama Medical Center, if you don't mind."

"What's there?" he asked as soon as they were away from the airport. "Another meeting?"

"Just to pay my respects." They drove along in silence for a few minutes. "Ken, can we stop so I can get some flowers?"

When they were close to the hospital, Ken spotted a young girl selling flowers on the street curb and pulled over to her. June got a cheerful-looking bunch of daisies before they continued on the last few blocks. She recognized the neighborhood as they got close. Leaning forward, she watched for what she wanted to see.

"Just stop at the curb and wait for a few minutes."

Once he found a place to park, she climbed out and went to the front entrance of the hospital. Off to one side, the garden area had recently been redone. A flagstone walkway led from the sidewalk to a private space separate from the rest of the garden. A small bamboo grove hid the area from general view, but once she was around the edge of the grove, she heard a small gurgling fountain. Following the stepping stones, she got to an area of lava rocks. Getting closer, she saw remnants of paint streaks on a few and tried to read them.

"Hayashi…Kealoha…Ramirez…Kulu…Kealoha again…Takatani…"

She stepped off the path and went to one side of the group of rocks, still scanning the hand-painted names.

"I don't see it. Nothing says Maile."

June poked around a bit more, the small bunch of flowers in one hand, her other hand wiping dirt and leaves from stones.

"Rats. I thought for sure she'd be here."

She went back to the pathway. Just as she was bending down to lay the flowers at another stone, she saw it.

She had been looking for Maile written with English words. What she saw, however, was Mari written in simple Japanese characters. It was the very first stone at the front. Using her free hand, she wiped dust and dirt away from the time-stained lava rock before setting the flowers at its base. She clasped her hands together and said a quick prayer before standing again.

"Okay, that takes care of that," she said quietly before turning back to Ken's waiting taxi.

■■■

About Kay Hadashi

Kay Hadashi is a former surgical nurse who turned to writing suspense and adventure novels, weaving medical drama into many of her plots. Third generation Japanese American and born and raised in Honolulu, her stories include strong women characters and are steeped with Hawaiian and Japanese culture. Most of her books span three generations of the Kato family, and the adventures they share. Hadashi has written more than twenty books and has contributed to several mystery short story anthologies.

David VanDyke, best-selling author of the Plague Wars and Stellar Conquest Series, calls her character June Kato, a 'kick-ass heroine'. Toby Neal, author of the Lei Crime Series, says, "Here's an author whose heroine mine should meet." She has also teamed with Nick Stephenson of the Leopold Blake private detective series to write "Ratio", a cross-over novel including both of their characters.

Readers who enjoy exciting stories filled with suspense and drama like Hadashi's novels. From the thrills in the original suspense series, to the trials of a daring young woman in the Melanie Kato Adventures, the writing team at Kay Hadashi Novels hopes you find something fun to read!

Made in the USA
Middletown, DE
06 March 2023

26307391R00099